A THIEF OR TWO

Sara Woods

The jury, passing on the prisoner's life,
May in the sworn twelve have a thief or two
Guiltier than him they try.
Measure for Measure, Act II, scene i

ST. MARTIN'S
NEW YORK

All rights reserved. For information, write:
St. Martin's Press, Inc., 175 Fifth Ave., New York,
N.Y. 10010

Printed in Great Britain

Library of Congress Catalog Card Number: 77–76659

First published in the United States of America in
1977

Library of Congress Cataloging in Publication Data
Woods, Sara, pseud.
  A thief or two.

  I. Title
PZ4.W895Tgp (PR6073.063) 823'.9'14 77–76659
ISBN 0–312–79994–2

Any work of fiction whose characters were of uniform
excellence would rightly be condemned – by that fact
if by no other – as being incredibly dull. Therefore
no excuse can be considered necessary for the villainy
or folly of the people appearing in this book. It seems
extremely unlikely that any one of them should
resemble a real person, alive or dead. Any such
resemblance is completely unintentional and without
malice.

S.W.

THE CASE FOR THE PROSECUTION

THURSDAY, the first day of the trial

There was a stir among the spectators in the court-room as Counsel for the Prosecution, having finished his opening address, gathered his gown about him and seated himself with a marked air of satisfaction. Mr. Justice Conroy, who had a sharp eye for any disturbance, directed a severe look in their direction, but evidently decided that the bounds of decorum were not on this occasion to be infringed. He settled himself, therefore, more comfortably in his place, and looked out over his domain with the eye of long experience.

Altogether, he could promise himself a certain amount of amusement, if only from the contrasting characters of the two leading counsel. There was Paul Garfield, for instance, appearing for the Crown; a precise man, a careful man, almost handsome in spite of a bony, enquiring, over-prominent nose. A Puritan if ever there was one. And there was Antony Maitland, for the defence; taller than his opponent, with a casual air and a humorous look that might have caused some qualms in a man less self-assured than Conroy. He had a reputation, too, for being, on occasion, rather less than orthodox; well, the judge could deal with that, too, if it arose. There had been a time, eight years ago . . .

Well, that had ended in a victory for the defence, with Garfield a little ungraciously acknowledging the justice of the fact that the case had been dismissed without even going to the jury. This time, perhaps . . . outlined with Garfield's precision it had sounded a strong case, but who was to know what surprises the defence might have in store. The accused now . . . some little clerk, thought Mr. Justice Conroy with unconscious arrogance. Or . . . no, that wasn't quite right, an assistant in a jeweller's shop. He was accused of theft, as well as murder, and in all honesty he didn't look the man to carry out either offence. But then, if there was one thing his years on the bench had taught him it was not to judge by appearances. A small man, the prisoner, with sandy hair well sleeked down and regular features that might almost have been considered handsome if he had had more presence. Well, time would tell, time would tell. There was the first witness now, to claim his attention.

The first witness was a man of middle height who had a well-fed look about him without being actually obese. He was very dark, bespectacled, with a round, amiable face and an incongruously jutting chin. He gave his name as Henry DeLisle, and admitted, in answer to Garfield's question, to being the brother of the deceased.

'Now, Mr. DeLisle, may I ask you to be kind enough to cast your mind back to Saturday, the thirteenth day of June last.' Maitland, who might have been asleep during the opening address for all anyone could tell, was paying more attention now, and Garfield was obviously choosing his words with care. 'Did you go to your shop that morning?'

'My – er – establishment,' corrected the witness, firmly but without animosity. 'I was not responsible for the day-to-day running of the business. My brother George, heaven rest his soul, attended to all that.'

'The deceased being responsible for the business side of the partnership – ' began Garfield, who had a passion for accuracy, but Henry DeLisle interrupted him, quite gently, before he could get any further.

'DeLisle Brothers, Jewellers. I myself am responsible for whatever artistic merit there is in our designs.'

Maitland exchanged a smile with his junior, Derek Stringer. The witness might be an artist, as he claimed, but obviously he had an eye for the advantages of advertising too.

'Yes, that is very clear,' said Garfield approvingly. Probably he had not expected so much clarity from the artistic temperament. 'The deceased, however – '

'My brother George,' said the witness sorrowfully. 'I cannot imagine how I shall get along without him.' It was doubtful, Maitland thought, that he was deliberately trying to provoke Counsel for the Prosecution, but if he went on this way he would undoubtedly succeed. 'No, on that particular Saturday morning he did not go into town. Our staff were competent,' – for a moment his glance flickered towards the man in the dock – 'we thought they were trustworthy, there was no need – ' He spread his hands, and let the sentence trail into silence.

'No, precisely. Before we go any further, Mr. DeLisle, will you describe for us your household? You have given us your address. That is one of the big houses not far from Wimbledon Common, is it not?'

'That is correct. George and I owned the house jointly, until on his death his share reverted to me. He was a bachelor. I am married, and my wife, of course, also lives there. Our two children are married, and have left home.'

'So there were living in the house your wife, Mrs. Grace DeLisle, yourself, Mr. George DeLisle – '

'Our butler, Canning; a housemaid, Maud; and the cook, Mrs. Canning.'

'Thank you. But on this particular weekend you had plans, had you not, to entertain?'

'Yes, rather a large party.'

'Will you tell us – ?' This time it was Garfield himself who left the sentence uncompleted.

7

'The – I think I may say the guest of honour was Sir Leonard Bowling. And Lady Bowling, of course. For his convenience we had arranged to display some of our most choice pieces at our home that evening.'

'And the rest of the party – '

'Mr. and Mrs. William Wyatt, who are friends of the family, had expressed an interest in seeing what we had to offer. With them came their daughter, Eleanor. Two other bachelor members of the party, who were coming only to dinner, owed their invitations to her. Laurence Blake is engaged to her, and Godfrey Thurlow, who is an antique dealer, employs her.'

'You have not yet told us, Mr. DeLisle, how the accused came to be a member of the party.'

'Harte – Malcolm Harte, the accused – ' said the witness, who seemed to have become infected with some of Garfield's passion for precision, 'was employed in our establishment as a salesman. George had arranged for him to bring the jewellery I mentioned to the house that day, and my wife, Grace – mistakenly as I see now – had invited him to stay over the Saturday night.'

'Why was that?'

'He is perfectly presentable,' said the witness a little huffily, as though that had somehow been called in question.

'But the reason, Mr. DeLisle,' Garfield insisted.

'Out of the kindness of her heart.' He did not sound as if he had much sympathy with this. 'She also asked my secretary, Mary Reynolds, who is, or was, engaged to him. Said the poor young things had very little chance of being alone together.' (Perhaps, thought Maitland, his scornful tone wasn't altogether to be wondered at. A crowded house such as he had described could hardly have afforded many opportunities to even the most ingenious of lovers.)

Garfield smiled a rather wintry smile; it could not, in

8

any case, have been called sympathetic. 'That, then, is the whole party, Mr. DeLisle?'

'It is.'

'Then will you describe for us the events of that day. From the time, say, that the accused arrived at the house.'

'I will do my best. Harte arrived at about two o'clock, while we were still taking coffee after lunch. He had the cases containing the jewellery in an attaché case. I took this from him and went directly to the study, where I put the individual jewel cases into the safe.'

'Locking the safe?'

'Why, naturally.'

'And the attaché case?'

'That was left standing by the wall nearby.'

'Was the jewellery the only thing that the prisoner brought to Wimbledon?'

'No. I should explain that the settings were not precisely antique, but a little old-fashioned. Sir Leonard had expressed an interest in something more modern. There were therefore sketches of my new designs, which were also in the attaché case, and which were also put in the safe.'

'Being original, and therefore valuable.'

'Of course.'

'And after you had put away the jewellery and your new designs – ?'

'I joined the others in the lounge. Miss Reynolds had arrived with Harte, and my wife suggested that they might care to walk on the Common for a while. They went out, but were back in time for tea at five o'clock. Sir Leonard and Lady Bowling had arrived by that time, and the Wyatts came at about half past six. Mr. Thurlow and Mr. Blake, who, as I told you, were only asked for dinner, arrived within a few minutes of each other at about a quarter to eight.'

'By which time, I suppose, the whole party were gathered together.'

'In the lounge, yes. Dinner was at eight-thirty, and we didn't hurry ourselves. At ten o'clock, back again in the lounge, George went to fetch the jewellery.'

'The whole party being there to view it?'

'Yes, though Harte and Miss Reynolds, being familiar with the pieces already, did not display much interest.'

'This might be a good time, Mr. DeLisle, to describe what was there, and give us some estimate of the total value.'

'There was a tiara. I understood from Lady Bowling that she had no use for it in that form, but the stones were beautiful.'

'The stones?'

'Diamonds.'

'And in addition to that – ?'

'Two pendants. One again in diamonds only, a tear-drop shape with one large stone and twelve small but perfect stones surrounding it. The other of diamonds and emeralds; I used the stones in my new designs, but quite frankly for that one piece I should have liked them to be retained in their old setting. There are photographs – '

'We will come to those in a minute, Mr. DeLisle.'

'Then you will see for yourself,' the witness promised. 'Though, of course, no photograph can give you a real impression of the quality of the stones.'

'You were giving us a list of the jewellery the prisoner brought to your home on June thirteenth,' Garfield reminded him.

'Yes. There were two bracelets, emeralds and diamonds; a brooch, an emerald in a filigree setting. I should explain that Sir Leonard was particularly interested in emeralds. Lady Bowling has very beautiful red hair, the true Titian colour.'

Garfield coughed. Really, you had to applaud his restraint, Maitland reflected, and saw from the corner of his eye that Stringer was smiling to himself, obviously echoing his thought. 'The list, Mr. DeLisle,' Counsel for the Prosecution prompted gently.

'It is nearly ended. A *fourche* in – '

'A *fourche*?' queried the judge, raising his head and looking at the witness over the top of his glasses.

'Literally, a fork, my lord,' Garfield told him. 'A kind of a comb, as I understand it, for the hair.'

'An ornament?' Conroy insisted, turning his attention to counsel.

'Yes, my lord.'

'Thank you, Mr. Garfield. You may proceed.'

'Mr. DeLisle. A *fourche*, you said.'

'In translucent enamels and emeralds. Of course, as I am sure you realise, Lady Bowling had no use for it in that form – '

'That does not concern us,' said Garfield, with the first sign of impatience he had shown.

'The same comment applies to the final item on the list,' said the witness, unabashed. 'There was also a bolero, in diamonds and other precious stones which I could use in my designs. To be precise – '

'Thank you, Mr. DeLisle. As you reminded me, there are the photographs. May I introduce into evidence, my lord . . . '

There was an interval while the photographs were produced and studied. Maitland allowed his attention to wander to the jury; there was a young woman in the front row who might have looked well in emeralds herself. He wondered if the thought occurred to her as she bent her head over the glossy enlargements. The stout woman beside her did no more than glance at the pictures before she passed them on. The witness waited serenely; an unusual man, if a tiresome one, with apparently no trace of self-consciousness.

'Now, Mr. DeLisle,' said Garfield at last. 'We come to the question of the value of the pieces you have described.'

'If they could have been sold as they are at present – I should say, as they were that day, for certainly the thieves would not retain them in that form – about £70,000. For the stones alone, which is the price I quoted to Sir Leonard, £50,000.'

'A valuable haul, then.'

'A damnable business,' said Henry DeLisle, with the first sign of emotion he had shown.

Garfield coughed again, and glanced at the judge, who did not, however, catch his eye. 'We come then to the events of that Saturday evening,' he said. 'Saturday, the thirteenth of June.' He glanced at the jury-box, to see whether any of its members showed signs of having registered this fact... but for all you could tell from their expressions, thought Maitland, none of them might have any intelligence at all. Perhaps the careful emphasis Garfield placed on each fact in turn might have some merit, though to his mind his opponent indulged himself in repetition rather more than was strictly necessary. There was no doubt, though, who held the cards in this case. When it came to mounting a defence with only one witness, the accused himself, denying everything, you were in a fair way to being beaten from the start. Garfield knew that, of course, but it wouldn't make any difference to his presentation, he was making that clear. His opening address had been a model of lucidity, and the devil of it was, he was probably right. Malcolm Harte was a likeable fellow, but that, unfortunately, was no guarantee of innocence. But he ought to be attending . . .

'You had reached ten o'clock, Mr. DeLisle,' said Garfield encouragingly. 'The whole party was present in the drawing-room, and your brother had gone to fetch the jewellery.'

'The jewellery and the sketches. About half an hour later – '

'What happened during that half-hour?'

'There was . . . well, a sort of general viewing first, with the pieces passing from hand to hand. Harte and Miss Reynolds were talking by the window.'

'But the accused would, as a member of your staff and the person who brought the jewellery to the house, be perfectly familiar with what was on show.'

'Certainly he would.'

'And with its value.'

'Of course.'

'Thank you, Mr. DeLisle. I am sorry to have interrupted you.' Garfield, getting what he wanted, was smooth as silk again.

'Then, after everyone had had an opportunity to see and exclaim over the beauty of the stones – and to be amused, in the case of the ladies, by some of the pieces – I showed my sketches and gave Sir Leonard and Lady Bowling a chance to consider them. I think I may say they were pleased with what they saw – '

'I am sure of that.' A slight tinge of tartness in Garfield's tone now. 'And at the end of the half-hour – '

'George took the various items back to the study.'

'And remained there?'

'Yes.'

'Why was that?'

'He said he had letters to write, but I believe myself it was to avoid refusing a nightcap, which he knew I should offer our guests. He wasn't teetotal, you understand, but he said that drinking late at night kept him awake.'

'And this was at ten-thirty, more or less?'

'Almost exactly ten-thirty, because just after he had

gone Mr. Thurlow looked at his watch and exclaimed about the time, and he and Mr. Blake both left within the next five minutes.'

'And what happened then?'

'The ladies retired – '

'That is Mrs. Grace DeLisle, Lady Bowling, Mrs. Rose Wyatt and her daughter Eleanor, and Miss Mary Reynolds.'

'That is correct. Harte went up at the same time. I must say I was relieved at that. He hardly fitted in.'

'That left yourself, Mr. Wyatt, and Sir Leonard Bowling in the drawing-room.'

'It did. As George had foreseen, I rang for Canning and he brought the decanters.'

'And after that?'

'We remained in the lounge, talking, the three of us, for about an hour.'

'Can you not remember the time more precisely, Mr. DeLisle?'

'I think it was eleven-thirty when we went up to bed, but I can't swear to that.'

'Very well, your impression must suffice. Now I must ask you to go into some detail as to your movements after that.'

'My wife was asleep. I was as quiet as I could be over my preparations for retiring, and when I was ready – '

'Again I must ask you to be more specific as to the time.'

'I can tell you, I think, because I know I phoned the police at eleven fifty-five, and it must have been five minutes before that that I put on my dressing-gown and went along to my brother's room.'

'Eleven-fifty then?'

'Yes. I expected him to be there, of course, there could have been nothing to keep him in the study for so long, but the bed was still as the maid had left it when she turned it down.'

'What did you think when you saw that?'

'I thought perhaps he had fallen asleep downstairs. So, as I wanted a word with him, I went down myself and found him . . . dead.'

'This must be distressing for you, Mr. DeLisle.' Garfield's voice was completely devoid of sympathy. 'Even so, I should like you to tell us, if you will, exactly what you found in the study.'

'My brother George was in his chair by the fireplace. His right temple, the whole of that side of his head, was smashed. I did not take it in immediately, but there was a large crystal of uncut amethyst lying on the floor at his side. It usually stood on the desk for use as a paperweight. It looked as if Harte had snatched it up and hit out wildly.'

'My lord!' Maitland was on his feet. 'My learned friend will agree with me that that is a most improper remark.'

'Certainly, my lord,' said Garfield, without waiting for Conroy's ruling. 'Mr. DeLisle, the case has not yet been tried.'

The witness took the rebuke with no outward show of emotion, though his expression seemed to say that this was only a formality. He knew what he knew. Maitland, seating himself, glanced at his client; funny how the man seemed to combine almost classical good looks with an insignificant personality. Now he saw that a touch of colour had crept into the pale cheeks. Malcolm Harte was looking at the witness, and just for the moment his eyes were bright with anger and he didn't look insignificant at all. But then the spark died and there was no more to be seen than he had seen earlier, a man very much afraid.

'Leaving aside matters of opinion,' Garfield was

saying, 'will you tell us what you saw in the study?'

'It took me a moment to take it in, that he was dead,' said Henry DeLisle, still calmly. 'Then, of course, I looked around, and saw the amethyst paperweight, as I told you. My sketches were still spread about the desk, but the safe was open and empty. I called the police and our doctor before I did anything else, though it was obvious there was nothing to be done for George. Then I made a superficial search of the room, but the pieces of jewellery we had displayed to our guests earlier were nowhere to be found.'

'One more thing, Mr. DeLisle. The accused has made a statement – '

'One moment, Mr. Garfield.' The judge looked up from his note-taking. 'Have you any objection to make, Mr. Maitland, as to the introduction of the statement your client made to the police?'

'No objection at all, my lord. It is the simple truth.' (And that I doubt, but according to my instructions . . .)

'The accused has made a statement,' said Garfield, taking up where he left off, 'that he spent ten minutes in the study after he had ostensibly retired – '

'My lord!'

'Yes, Mr. Maitland.'

'I cannot allow the implication to pass unchallenged that there was any element of deceit in my client's conduct. He *had* retired, but went downstairs again upon an impulse.'

'Very well, Mr. Maitland. Perhaps you will rephrase your question, Mr. Garfield.'

'As your lordship pleases.' If counsel was weary of repeating himself, no one could have told it. 'The accused has made a statement that he spent ten minutes with your brother in the study, from about ten-forty to ten-fifty, at the end of which period Mr. George DeLisle asked him to put the jewel cases into the safe. Do you think this is likely?'

'I must protest, my lord,' said Maitland, coming to his feet in a hurry. But this time he was too late, the witness spoke through his objection, saying clearly:

'From my knowledge of my brother, I should say it was completely out of character.'

The answer was not allowed to stand in the record, but what good was that? The jury had heard it. And Garfield was continuing, completely unperturbed by the slight altercation. 'One further point, Mr. DeLisle. Did the prisoner know the combination of the safe?'

'He had no need to know it, no right to know it. But I cannot rule out the possibility – '

'How is that, Mr. DeLisle?'

'I kept a note of it in my desk.'

'Your desk at the establishment in Bourne Lane?'

'Yes. Not that I often use it, of course, being more often at the drawing-board. But it is certainly possible that Harte saw it there. And, as he knew the combination of the strong-room, he would be in little doubt as to what these other figures referred.'

While this exchange had been going on, Stringer had glanced in some surprise at his leader. But Maitland did no more than shake his head slightly at the enquiry in his junior's look, and muttered under his breath, 'What is cross-examination for, after all?'

'It will perhaps be relevant here, Mr. DeLisle,' Garfield was continuing, 'to ask you about your connections in the jewellery trade in Amsterdam.'

'We have a widespread knowledge of dealers there, both for buying and selling stones,' said Henry complacently.

'Would it be reasonable to say that the accused shared this knowledge?'

17

'Certainly. He has been in our – in my employ for nearly seven years.'

'And therefore might not have been altogether at a loss to dispose of jewellery on his own account.'

'My lord!' said Maitland, interrupting suddenly. 'The witness is being called upon for altogether too much speculation.'

'Yes, Mr. Garfield,' said Conroy, who seemed, however, to give the ruling with reluctance, 'in this case I must agree with the defence.'

And perhaps, after all, I was wrong to intervene, thought Maitland, seating himself. The implication had been made, and the jury would have noted it.

Garfield probably realised that only too well, at any rate he went on smoothly. 'There is one other point, Mr. DeLisle – and again I am referring to the prisoner's statement, my lord – there is one other point on which I should like clarification. Had Mr. George DeLisle spoken to you about the possible cancellation of Malcolm Harte's holiday.'

'No. He had not.' Henry DeLisle sounded puzzled.

'Can you conceive of any reason why this should have been done?'

'None whatever.'

'Then I must ask you . . . I am sorry, Mr. DeLisle, I know you find this distressing,' – his voice was as coldly unsympathetic as ever (was that what made him so formidable an opponent, that he was above displaying any ordinary human feelings?) – 'but I'm afraid we must go back over one or two points, just to make it quite clear to the jury . . . '

The foreman of the jury was a thin, sharp-featured man who looked like a schoolmaster and was, in fact, the owner of a small chain of grocery stores. If Maitland had known that he would certainly have quoted Chesterton on the subject of grocers, and the foreman himself would have seen nothing humorous in the accusations, being almost completely without a sense of the ridiculous. Up to this point he had been paying attention conscientiously enough, to the formalities at the beginning of the trial, with which he had previously been unfamiliar; to Garfield's opening address, which had impressed him to a degree that would have depressed Counsel for the Defence considerably; and now to this first witness. But by now, he thought, he had got a very fair idea of what had happened on the evening of the thirteenth of June. He was hardly aware that his mind was drifting away from the stuffy courtroom – the judge, perhaps forgivably on that bleak November day, had a morbid fear of draughts – but he would not in any case have felt it worth while to recall it merely to hear a repetition of Henry DeLisle's evidence. The prisoner, who looked a sickly sort of chap, was obviously guilty, or what was he doing here?

That had been an ugly scene yesterday, and quite unjustified in spite of what Belle had said afterwards. But then, Anne had always been possessive from a girl, he had known that, hadn't he, and taken it into consideration when he made his decision? And there had been nothing wrong in what he had done, all strictly legal and according to the law of the land. If Cousin Bert had wanted Anne to benefit from his dying he should have thought of it before, and not left word with his housekeeper (hearsay evidence only) of what he wished to be done. Well, there had been a nice legacy for Anne, £5,000, and the residue to himself. Which was as it should be; a man with a wife and family to support had more need of this world's goods than his spinster sister.

So Cousin Bert's goods and chattels had been his to dispose of, and a sorry lot they were to his taste, though one or two nice pieces that had fetched a good sum at the sale rooms. Give him something modern any day. Anne had asked for the pie-crust table, but he'd told her straight she'd have to buy it from the estate and she'd gone off in a huff. She hadn't mentioned the tea service until later, after the housekeeper had been talking to her.

19

And what business was it of hers once she had told him, as executor, what Cousin Bert had said on his death bed. If she could be believed, a mischief-maker, there was no doubt about it. Of course, when Anne approached him he said, 'No,' again. 'There's no proof,' he'd said, 'that Cousin Bert meant you to have it.' 'Only the housekeeper's word,' she'd said, 'and why should she lie about it?' 'Out of spite, I wouldn't wonder,' he'd said, and that should have been the end of it. £1,000 or more it was worth, Spode china made to a restricted design over a hundred years before, still the complete set, unchipped, twelve of everything. He couldn't have seen his way to letting it go on a mere rumour, even if Belle hadn't taken a liking to it. It had no place, really, in a modern flat, but nobody could say he wasn't an indulgent husband, and he'd done quite nicely out of Cousin Bert's legacy, thank you; and in any case, if Belle grew tired of it, it would still be saleable in a year or two's time.

But there'd been no call for Anne to come to the flat and make a scene, as she had yesterday. What use had she for twelve of everything, a spinster with very few friends? He'd said that, getting impatient with her complaints, and that had fairly set her off. 'You've no right to it,' she'd screamed at them. 'As for your friends, they only come for the booze, they'll not come twice if you offer them tea.' Well, he could hold his own in a slanging match any day, he flattered himself he'd given as good as he got except for one thing that rankled. 'Avaricious,' she'd said, and seemed pleased with the word. 'I never thought to see a brother of mine so avaricious.' It wasn't right, when Cousin Bert's will had been so clear, and probated by the courts, he'd pointed that out to her; but she was beside herself by that time, and wouldn't listen, and stormed out in the middle of what he was saying. She wouldn't come back in a hurry, he'd see to that, in spite of Belle seeming to sympathise a bit. 'If she really wants it,' she'd said, and he'd pointed out Anne wasn't concerned at all with its beauty, but only with what she might get for it. 'But if it's what Cousin Bert wanted,' Belle said, and he'd told her straight there was no proof of that.

That chap Harte now, it was easy enough to see the tempta-
tion. Working among all those valuable things day after day . . .
beautiful too, he supposed, to some people, perhaps Harte was
one of those. He wanted to get married, as Counsel for the Pro-
secution had told them, and on a ridiculously small salary; he'd
managed himself on less when he was young, but today's young
people they wanted everything, right off. And comparing himself
with the DeLisle Brothers, with their fine house and all, young
Harte had got to making comparisons. And see where that had
led him. Robbery and murder, there was no excuse for that.

The witness was a bit of a stuffed shirt, wasn't he? Abso-
lutely sure of himself and his place in the scheme of things. Belle
sometimes looked at the advertisements in the newspaper –
Jewellery, Goldsmiths and Silversmiths – *she'd like to*
deck herself out, no doubt, though she'd never absolutely said so.
And even if she did, with inflation what it was . . .

Garfield was seating himself and that other chap – Maitland,
the judge had called him – was getting to his feet. In spite of
what had gone before he had a confident air, but that was pure
play-acting, like as not. There'd been bits in the papers about
him, now and then; they even sometimes called him 'the man who
never loses a case', but that couldn't possibly be true. Well, he'd
have to pull a trick or two to win this one, with the prisoner so
obviously guilty, the motive staring you in the face. But, to start
with, it'd be interesting to see what he made of the witness.

THURSDAY, the first day (continued)

Maitland, rising to cross-examine, was as conscious
that opinion in the court was hardening against him as
he would have been if spectators and jury had joined
together in song like the chorus in *Trial by Jury*. He
wasn't quite sure what had put that in his mind –

And therefore we haven't a scrap
Of sympathy with the defendant

– but it was a most inappropriate thought and he banished it dutifully. The witness was eyeing him complacently, he'd give something to prick the bubble of the man's self-esteem, but that was an inappropriate thought too, to say nothing of being uncharitable. If he couldn't keep his mind on his job he'd have done better to let Derek cross-examine in his place.

'I shan't detain you long, Mr. DeLisle,' he said. 'There are just a few questions.' He glanced down at his notes, but they were almost illegible, even to him. 'You have told us that my client did not show much interest when you were displaying the jewellery you were trying to sell.'

'He knew better than anybody else what was there, having brought it himself from the strong-room.'

'The strong-room at the shop?'

'At our establishment, yes.'

'But the rest of the party were interested in what you had to show. Can you remember if any of them showed an especial interest?'

'I don't believe . . . well, it was only natural. Sir Leonard and Lady Bowling, they were the purchasers, after all. And Mr. Thurlow, but he was as interested in the settings as he was in the stones, and didn't seem to see that in *my* settings they would have been displayed so much more beautifully.'

'Anyone else?'

Henry DeLisle smiled. 'My wife,' he said, rather as if in some way he had scored a point off counsel. There was a faint titter from somewhere at the back of the spectators' gallery, and Mr. Justice Conroy looked up, frowning.

'I see.' Maitland was unmoved. 'A thing I should

like to know, Mr. DeLisle, is why you went to your brother's room that evening.'

'To . . . well, I suppose really because I was pleased with the prospect of selling the jewellery and wanted to congratulate him. As I explained, he attended to all the business details.'

'But surely your new designs had played almost as great a part – '

'Indeed, yes. I just wanted to talk things over with him.'

'Had the deal been completed?'

'The sale to Sir Leonard? No. But he had indicated his intention of buying, and I think he realised that our price was reasonable.'

'Did he indeed? Now, Mr. DeLisle, there is the question of the combination of the safe in the study at your home.'

'Yes?'

'You have intimated that it is possible that my client knew it.'

'Certainly.'

'The only way he could have done so would have been to go into your office and rummage through the papers in your desk?'

'That is so, but – '

'On the offchance that he might find it written down there. Had you ever said anything to make him think that was so?'

'He knows I have a very poor memory for figures.'

'Answer the question, please, Mr. DeLisle. Had you ever said anything to make him think he might find the combination written down on a piece of paper in your desk?'

'Well, if you put it like that, no, I hadn't, of course. There was no need for him to know it.'

'And have you any reason to believe that your papers had been tampered with at any time?'

'It is possible – '

'Any reason, Mr. DeLisle?'

'No.'

'Then we will turn to the other matter on which my friend invited you to speculate. The question of the possibility of my client having dealings of his own with firms in Amsterdam.'

'I was not permitted to proceed with this subject, my lord,' Garfield pointed out.

'Nevertheless, Mr. Garfield, I think it will be proper to allow the defence a little latitude.'

'Thank you, your lordship.' (You never know, I may dig my own grave.) Maitland turned to the witness again. 'I am sure, Mr. DeLisle, that any dealings you had with firms at home and abroad were strictly legitimate.'

'Of course.'

'Then it is unlikely, is it not, that through his association with your firm my client could have gained any knowledge that would assist him in disposing of stolen goods?'

The witness hesitated over that. (He genuinely thinks Harte guilty, and doesn't want to say anything that may help him to get away with it. All the same . . .) 'I must agree with you, it is unlikely,' said Henry DeLisle, with much less assurance than he had previously displayed.

'Thank you.' Perhaps it might help, and perhaps it mightn't. Change the subject then, before the witness could be inspired to add anything that might weaken the effect. 'You have told us, Mr. DeLisle, that your brother dealt with the business side of your joint affairs. Did that include matters concerning personnel?'

'It did.'

'You cannot be surprised then that he had not advised you of his intention of asking my client to change his holiday arrangements.'

'No, not really.'

'A simple matter of office routine.'

'I suppose so, but I can see no reason – '

'That does not concern us. Let us go back to the night of the tragedy. You have said there was nothing to keep Mr. George DeLisle in the study. What about the letters he said he was going to write?'

'As I said, I thought they were a – a polite fiction. Maybe, even, he had not had time to start. But my designs were spread about the desk, there was no sign that he had been writing.'

'I see. And the safe was open and empty?'

'As I have said.'

'The first thing that occurred to you was that there had been a theft of the jewellery?'

'That is true, yes.'

'One last point then. You were in the drawing-room with your friends from approximately ten-thirty to approximately eleven-thirty. Or, as you have called it, "the lounge". That is what you meant, is it not?'

'Certainly. My wife prefers that term.'

'So I must ask you, during that time did you hear anything from the study?'

'Nothing at all. The rooms are at opposite sides of the hall – '

'No doubt my friend has a plan for us.'

'Have you, Mr. Garfield?' asked the judge.

'It will be produced and sworn to by the next witness, my lord.'

'Admirable. I am sure you will be content to proceed in its absence for the moment, Mr. Maitland.'

'As your lordship pleases. You think then that you would not have heard anything that went on in the study, Mr. DeLisle?'

'I should have been very much surprised to have done so.'

'Any sound from the hall then . . . footsteps . . . a door closing?'

'Nothing.' The witness paused, and then was inspired to add, incautiously. 'The house is well built, and I do not suppose Harte was anxious to advertise his presence.'

'My lord!' said Maitland, more in sorrow than in anger, but Garfield was on his feet before the judge could speak.

'Mr. DeLisle, I have pointed out to you before that the question of the prisoner's guilt or innocence will be decided in due course by the jury. So far – '

'But when he admits himself – '

'You mustn't argue with counsel, Mr. DeLisle,' said the judge, shaking his head in an admonitory way.

'No, your lordship,' said the witness, not visibly chastened.

'Mr. Maitland – '

'Thank you, my lord.' He turned again to the witness. 'Did you leave the drawing-room – I beg your pardon, the lounge – at any time during the hour you spent there with Sir Leonard Bowling and Mr. William Wyatt?'

'I do not recollect . . . I am quite sure that I did not.'

'Then did either of your companions – ?'

'Both of them, at one time or another. But I cannot see – '

'It is not – forgive me – your concern.'

'No,' said Henry DeLisle, and for the first time sounded a little doubtful.

'Can you remember the time, or the duration of these absences?'

'Certainly not!' He made it sound, thought Maitland, suddenly amused, as though the suggestion was somehow an improper one.

'Then you cannot say but that either of these two gentlemen might have had time to go into the study?'

'I imagine their purpose was to visit the downstairs cloakroom,' said the witness huffily. 'But I remember, now I think of it, that Sir Leonard was the first one to absent himself, and that Mr. Wyatt went out only a few minutes before we all went upstairs.'

'But you cannot remember how long . . . no, precisely. Of course, you yourself could have gone downstairs again after you had retired . . . did, in fact, go downstairs again.'

'My lord!' Garfield sounded outraged.

'Yes, Mr. Maitland, I really do not feel – '

'I have learned so much from my learned friend's opening address,' said Maitland quickly, 'as to know that the prosecution are relying heavily on opportunity. If I can establish – '

'Very well, Mr. Maitland, very well! But I think you have already made your point, and can have no excuse for further questioning on these lines.'

'As your lordship pleases.' Counsel's tone was very faintly mutinous. If Conroy was going to be touchy on that point he'd be in difficulties when the other witnesses came on. Because there wasn't much to be said in Malcolm Harte's favour . . . 'I have no further questions,' he added, and sat down with a swirl of his gown.

'Have you any further questions for the witness, Mr. Garfield?'

'No, my lord, I have not. Thank you, Mr. DeLisle.' The witness glanced a little uncertainly at the judge, and then stepped down, to be taken in tow by the usher.

'The court will recess until two o'clock,' said the judge, with ill-concealed satisfaction.

Maitland took Derek Stringer, and their instructing solicitor, Geoffrey Horton, to lunch at Astroff's, where

27

he knew they could get served quickly if necessary, as it was today. 'Garfield,' said Derek, laying his menu aside and addressing himself to his drink, 'was most damnably convincing.'

'Must you remind me?'

'Well, I don't see . . . we really haven't any sort of a case at all, you know.'

'I've given you everything I could,' said Geoffrey defensively. He was slightly younger than his two companions, who were much of an age, though Stringer looked the elder; Horton had red hair and a normally cheerful disposition, and no more simple faith than was proper for a man in his profession. But this time he had made up his mind, and was clinging to the opinion stubbornly, that his client was telling the truth.

'Of course you have. But I really don't see,' said Maitland in a reflective tone, 'why you wanted to involve me in the affair at all.'

'I told you, Antony, I think he's innocent. If you'd only listen – '

'I have listened to you . . . at length. I've also studied the prosecution's case, let alone hearing what Garfield had to say this morning, and there isn't a thing – not one single, solitary thing, Geoffrey – to back up your conviction.'

'Only Harte's statement.'

'Come now! Short of pleading guilty, he had to say something. And he hasn't told us, let me remind you, why he went down to the study again.'

'He says he wanted to speak to George DeLisle about the leave he was taking for his honeymoon.'

'Yes, but why then? It sounds a manufactured excuse to me. What do you think, Derek?'

'I think we shall enjoy our lunch better if we forget about the trial for the moment,' said Derek pacifically, though conscious as he spoke that he was the one who had introduced the subject. But neither of the others reminded him of that fact, and the rest of the meal passed without further argument.

After the luncheon recess there was a procession of witnesses, beginning, as promised, with the man who produced a plan of the ground floor of the house in Wimbledon. The defence caused a slight delay here by demanding also a plan of the upper floor; Garfield couldn't see any reason why it should be wanted, but Maitland was persistent and, after hearing some argument, the judge decided to take his part. The plan had been made, the witness liked to do a job thoroughly, but he hadn't brought it to court. Press on, then, and let him be recalled later when the plan was in his possession.

'But I don't quite see why you want it,' said Derek, as his leader sat down again. Maitland was smiling.

'I don't know that I do,' he replied. 'But Geoffrey will account it a sign of grace, you can bet on that.'

'Are you coming round to his way of thinking then?' asked Stringer bluntly, but the next witness was already in the box, and Maitland only shook his head, his eyes intent.

It was hardly worth while cross-examining the finger-print expert. Stringer had one question only for him. 'You say, Mr. Brown, that you found Mr. Harte's fingerprints on the door of the safe. Was there anything about them inconsistent with the fact that he had opened the safe door and placed the jewel cases inside?'

'Nothing inconsistent,' said the witness doubtfully. 'But – '

'Thank you, Mr. Brown, you have answered my question. That is all.' But Garfield, in his careful way, had to underline his point.

'The fingerprints could equally well have been made

if the safe was opened to take something out.' (Well, that was obvious enough, no need to go on about it.)

'Yes, of course,' said the witness, and was allowed to go.

There were other police witnesses, who came and went in quick succession . . . the course of the enquiry . . . the arrest. Then the pathologist, who had more to say for himself, but it all boiled down to the fact that he was uncertain about the time of death. One limit was set by the fact that George DeLisle had been seen by the whole party, alive and well, at ten-thirty, but he might have been killed at any time up to eleven-thirty, or even later. Then he became extremely technical . . .

. . . and the second juror, who sat immediately on the left of the foreman, and who was squeamish about medical matters, found the whole thing both distasteful and dull. He was a younger man than his immediate neighbour, rather nattily dressed, and was employed by one of the big insurance companies as an investigator. That gave him a certain fellow feeling with the police, he flattered himself that he knew their problems. But this case seemed to be a pushover, as far as he was concerned they'd made their point as early as Garfield's opening speech. No need to listen carefully . . .

It was bad luck being called up for jury duty like this, meant a loss of income if a big fire came up or a jewel theft like the one this chap Harte had pulled off. Got clean away with the stuff too, in spite of being arrested so soon after the event. That meant professional help; hard luck on him really, they weren't likely to keep his share safe for him until he came out of prison. If he'd been cleverer, but he hadn't and that was that. No sympathy to waste for a careless operator.

That claim now, he could have made something out of it. He wondered who the DeLisle brothers had been insured with. If there'd been evidence of a fraud, of course, that was even better. Easy pickings. But even without that, the claim could always be adjusted. Henry DeLisle was a shrewd operator all right, he'd have been good for a thousand or two.

So he'd been called for jury duty, so he was missing opportunities, what of it? There'd be others. No need for Freddie to go near hysterical just because he'd told him they'd have to go carefully for a bit, live on his salary which he didn't consider over-generous. If he hadn't bought the mews cottage there'd have been plenty in the kitty, but he had and that was that. Freddie had been as willing that he should purchase it as he had been himself, hardly fair that he should turn on him now. But there was no denying it, Freddie could be difficult. He was getting too sure of himself, too sure of his influence, too sure of the money that rolled in from time to time. But it had been a mistake telling him where it came from, made it difficult to make a break if ever he should want to. Not that he did, of course, Freddie suited him. But one should always consider future possibilities.

That was the mistake the prisoner had made, ought to feel some sympathy for the fellow, but murder was going a bit far. If he'd been reasonably careful about fingerprints, though, there might have been plenty of suspicion but no real proof. God, but this was boring. Perhaps after this doctor chap had finished the judge would call it a day.

But there was one more witness to be heard before they adjourned, the architect who had returned with the plan of the first floor of the DeLisles' house. Introducing it didn't take long, however, Maitland expressed himself satisfied, and Mr. Justice Conroy called a temporary halt to the proceedings.

Antony Maitland and his wife, Jenny, had their own quarters at the top of Sir Nicholas Harding's house in Kempenfeldt Square. The arrangement had once been regarded as temporary, but was now hallowed by time, and though it had its disadvantages the advantages on the whole outweighed them. Sir Nicholas was Antony's uncle, and the head of the chambers in the Inner Temple to which he belonged, and though he was inclined to speak his mind upon occasion a little too freely there were conveniences, there could be no denying it, in being housed under the same roof.

Maitland spent a little time in chambers after the adjournment, but things were fairly well under control and his uncle had already left. It was still a little earlier than usual when he got home, but he wasn't surprised to find Gibbs hovering at the back of the hall. Gibbs was a disagreeable old man who insisted on retaining his post as Sir Nicholas's butler in spite of the united efforts of the household to persuade him into retirement. His duties had gradually whittled themselves away to answering the door, and serving dinner when he felt like it, and he always – to everyone's relief – retired promptly at ten o'clock; but somehow he almost always managed to be in the hall when Antony came in, making his presence and his disapproval felt. He disapproved of most things, you had to give him that, but of his employer's nephew in particular, regarding him as a disruptive influence; and the years that had passed since Antony joined the household soon after his thirteenth birthday had done nothing to reconcile the old man to his presence. So when he said now, 'Sir Nicholas is dining with you, Mr. Maitland,' it was in doom-laden tones, as though the change of plan had personally affected him in some way, and was all Antony's fault into the bargain. Or it might be, with his capacity for fearing the worst, thought Antony, allowing amusement to get the better of irritation, that he thinks Uncle Nick will die horribly as the result of eating some careless concoction of mushrooms. Something like that. Or, on second thoughts, just possibly not. He had sometimes thought that if Gibbs liked anybody in this world it was Jenny.

But he only said, 'That's good,' in a non-committal tone; and then, 'Good night, Gibbs,' as he made for the stairs.

As it wasn't Tuesday, when Sir Nicholas generally joined them – escaping the horrors of the cold collation his housekeeper would have left for him while she went to the pictures – there was a minor mystery here. It was solved by Jenny, who came out into the hall as soon as she heard him. 'He's curious about the murder trial, Antony,' she told him, as he shrugged out of his overcoat and threw it on the nearest chair. 'So I thought I'd better ask him to stay.'

'Heaven forbid that we should send him away in any way unsatisfied,' said Antony piously. 'But I can't see, Uncle Nick, why you should be interested,' he added, as they went into the living-room together. 'It's all very dull.'

Sir Nicholas picked up his sherry glass and looked at his nephew over the rim. They were much of a height, though the older man was more heavily built, with hair too fair to show that it was greying and an unconscious air of authority. 'Come now,' he said in encouraging tones. 'A real-life drama, according to the press. Besides – '

'Besides what?' asked Antony, making for the writing-table where the tray with the decanter had been placed.

'There is, besides, the juxtaposition of yourself with Garfield,' said Sir Nicholas placidly. He sipped, and replaced his glass. '*The words of Mercury are harsh,*' he went on, '*after the songs of Apollo.*'

'No, really, Uncle Nick,' – for a moment Maitland was genuinely annoyed – 'there's no need to dig that up again.'

'The *Clarion* have done so.'

'Damn them!'

'I saw that,' said Jenny, 'and it seemed to ring a bell, only I can't quite remember – '

'That chap Harland, who could never speak without tagging on a quotation,' said Antony. 'He was my client, so of course I only asked him things we both wanted answered. But when Garfield took over to cross-examine, naturally he wasn't so gentle; the judge – it was Conroy that time, too – had occasion to rebuke Harland for not answering one of Garfield's questions, and that was the answer he got.'

Jenny laughed. She had gone back to her favourite corner of the sofa and curled up there in a way that Sir Nicholas, when out of temper, had occasionally told her was undignified. Her brown curls shone gold in the lamplight, and her clear grey eyes, as they met her husband's, were brimming with amusement. 'I think it's apt enough to be funny,' she said. 'You can't blame them for remembering it.'

'Can't I?' he grumbled. But Jenny's laughter was infectious, he was smiling as he came round Sir Nicholas's chair to take up his stand on the hearth-rug, his glass on the mantel, which also provided a convenient prop for his shoulder. 'Anyway, Uncle Nick, apart from wanting to dig up things better forgotten, what aspect of the case is attracting your attention.'

'You told me Horton thinks your client is innocent.'

'So he does. I don't. And that's only my opinion, Jenny,' he added quickly. 'He says he didn't commit either theft or murder, and I'm bound to give him the benefit of the doubt.'

Jenny, who had been known to argue with him in similar cases the ethics of his position, showed no sign of being about to do so on this occasion. Sir Nicholas said thoughtfully, 'You must admit it's an amusing reversal of the usual order. Of the two of you, Horton is generally the more sceptical.'

'Don't say I'm credulous, Uncle Nick.'

'Aren't you?' queried his uncle gently. Antony grinned.

'I'm not *always* wrong,' he pointed out. 'Anyway, in this instance – '

'Knowing Horton, I'm wondering how long you'll be able to withstand the temptation to meddle.'

'A bit late in the day for that, isn't it? The trial's already started.'

'There have been occasions in the past when that fact proved no deterrent.'

'Look here, are you trying to encourage me or discourage me, Uncle Nick?'

'Neither. I am just – '

'Amused by the situation. So you said.' He took his glass and went to sit in the chair opposite his uncle. 'Of course, Geoffrey's no fool.'

'I wondered how long it would be before you remembered that fact,' said Sir Nicholas, still maddeningly placid.

'It's quite a straightforward case.'

'Which Garfield is going to win.'

'I don't see how that can be helped. We've only one witness, Harte himself.'

'And if his story didn't convince you it's unlikely to convince the jury.'

'That's true, but – '

'I have it on good authority, Antony, that Garfield is out for blood.' Sir Nicholas interrupted him without apology. 'He hasn't forgotten the Harland case any more than the newspapers have. Or than you have yourself, I imagine.'

'But it was all perfectly clear. Garfield himself agreed – '

'Yes, he has a strong sense of justice, which is just what makes him so dangerous. He genuinely loathes the

35

crimes that have been committed and wants to see them punished. And if he ever reaches the bench I can't see him taking much account of extenuating circumstances.'

'We aren't talking about extenuating circumstances. We're talking about the possibility of Harte being innocent.'

'That was merely a remark in passing. The point is, Garfield can't have liked the Harland case, everything about it must have revolted him. The drama – '

'I didn't like it myself. But what did you mean, Uncle Nick, "on good authority".'

'Halloran had it from Appleby . . . who is Garfield's junior in this case,' Sir Nicholas added in an aside to Jenny, who was sipping her sherry and listening quietly to this exchange.

'Well, even if it's true, I don't see what I can do about it. He'll win the case, I'm expecting that, I can only do my best for my client with the material I've got.' He glanced at Jenny, and then back at his uncle again. 'I've lost cases before, it isn't the end of the world,' he said.

'That is undeniably true. Garfield will win his case, but what I'm afraid of, Antony, is that he will make a fool of you in the process.'

'But – ' He broke off, and took a moment to think that out. 'You're warning me against what you call meddling, Uncle Nick, because you think the case is hopeless anyway.'

'Precisely,' said his uncle in a commendatory tone.

'And if I start cross-examining with a view to uncovering a different culprit – '

'Are you quite sure you haven't already indulged yourself in something along those lines?'

'Quite sure.' But he thought about the plan of the

upstairs floor as he spoke, and the words trailed off uncertainly.

'You've thought of something,' said Sir Nicholas accusingly.

'Not really. No.' His intention had been, surely, merely the laudable one of annoying Garfield. Certainly he hadn't foreseen any future use for the plan. But he began to see what his uncle was getting at. 'I told you,' he protested, 'I haven't the slightest intention – '

'You have said so, certainly, but I have known you change your mind. And if you do – '

'The gypsy's warning,' said Antony irreverently. 'Have another drink, Uncle Nick, and let's forget about Garfield for a while.'

THURSDAY, the first day (continued)

It was a little after nine o'clock, while Jenny was clearing the table and Antony had gone to the cupboard to see if there was any brandy left, that Gibbs came toiling upstairs with the news that a Miss Wyatt had called, and wanted to see Mr. Maitland. (There was, of course, no need for him to do this, but he had boycotted the house telephone ever since it had been installed for his convenience.) 'I took the liberty of putting her in the study, Sir Nicholas, as she said it was a matter of business.'

'Wyatt . . . Wyatt?' said Sir Nicholas. 'Do you know any Wyatts, Antony?'

'No, but . . . did you say Miss or Mrs. Wyatt, Gibbs?'

'*Miss* Wyatt, Mr. Maitland.' In some way the query seemed to have offended the old man. 'A young lady,' he added huffily.

'Eleanor Wyatt, then. Damn, and damn.'

'A witness,' said Sir Nicholas, sitting up.

'No. She was there that weekend, but I don't think she has anything material to say about it. What do you suppose she wants?'

'To embroil you probably,' said Sir Nicholas mistrustfully.

'But . . . Geoffrey told me she was engaged to one of the men there, Laurence Blake. Nothing to do with Malcolm Harte at all.'

'Are you going to see her?'

'I suppose I must – '

'Or die of curiosity,' said his uncle disagreeably.

'May I use the study, Uncle Nick?'

'Not only may you use it, I will join you there,' said Sir Nicholas, getting up with alacrity. 'If you will forgive us, Jenny – '

'I'll keep the coffee hot until you come back,' said Jenny. There was a trace of uneasiness in her voice.

The study was a comfortable room, Sir Nicholas's favourite and the one he commonly used. To Antony's relief Gibbs had stoked up the fire, which must have been almost dead when the visitor arrived; that meant that the 'young lady' had met with some measure of approval in his eyes, however grudging. At least, she hadn't been left to freeze to death.

She was standing in the middle of the room, her attention apparently caught by the picture over the fire of Antony's grandfather, whom he had never known, but whom he secretly felt to be almost as disapproving of his presence in the house as Gibbs was. Eleanor was a tall girl, with fairish, straight hair that fell to her shoulders, a clear complexion, and – as could be seen when she spun round to face them – a troubled look in her eyes. Antony wasn't conscious of their colour in that first moment, but later he saw that they were of a shade that was nearer khaki than anything else. (Jenny said, 'That isn't really kind, Antony,' when he told her, but he countered that with, 'Very attractive.' And the odd thing was, that was right.)

'Are you – ?' She looked from Antony to his uncle, and then back again. 'You must be Mr. Maitland.'

'Yes, I am.'

'I'm Eleanor Wyatt. Is it . . . do you mind terribly my coming here like this?'

The truth was, he did mind, this kind of unconventional approach generally spelled trouble, but he could hardly tell her that. So he smiled at her and said, 'Not at all,' vaguely. And then, 'This is my uncle, Sir Nicholas Harding.'

At which Eleanor looked again at the older man and blurted, 'Oh, dear!' in a scared way.

Antony's smile broadened. He said lightly, 'He won't bite you, you know.'

'If you would prefer to see Mr. Maitland alone – ' Sir Nicholas suggested courteously. Which was a piece of pure humbug, as his nephew knew; when his curiosity was aroused it would take an atom bomb to shift him.

'No, of course . . . it's so difficult anyway,' said Eleanor Wyatt helplessly.

'Never mind. Sit down, Miss Wyatt . . . over there by the fire. And take your time,' Antony told her. He deserved credit for that, he wasn't feeling particularly patient.

She took the chair he had indicated, and Sir Nicholas seated himself in the big leather chair at the other side of the hearth, which was his own invariable choice. Antony, who would have liked to remain standing and free to move about the room, hesitated a moment and then pulled up the high-backed chair that stood against the wall by the door. The girl was nervous, probably she wouldn't like being loomed over.

And certainly she was in no hurry to speak, she was looking about her with interest, taking in the big, highly polished desk; the bookshelves, their contents none too neatly arranged; the window, heavily curtained in a moss-green material that had been Jenny's choice. Perhaps she would find some reassurance, on the whole it was a peaceful room, strangely at variance with its owner's rather turbulent character. Though just now, of course, he thought, looking at his uncle with a spurt of involuntary amusement, a child could have played with him.

But enough was enough. They couldn't wait all night. 'Miss Wyatt,' he said, leaning forward a little and trying to catch her eye, 'it would be helpful if you could tell me just why you're here.'

She looked him full in the face then, only too obviously trying to weigh him up. 'I've heard that you're good at puzzles, Mr. Maitland.'

That was the press, for whom he had very little love. 'I don't see quite where that takes us,' he said carefully, not wishing her to see his irritation.

'Well – I told you it was difficult – are you going to get Malcolm off?' she said.

The blunt question threw him off his guard. 'I can't discuss my client's affairs with you or anyone else,' he told her, and felt as he did so that he might have expressed himself with greater originality.

'I was afraid you'd say that,' she said, and sighed. 'You mean you think it's hopeless. Probably you don't even believe him.'

That was near enough the bone to keep him silent for a moment, and before he could think of anything to say Sir Nicholas spoke from the depths of his chair. 'I think it would be best, Miss Wyatt, if you were to tell us why you came here, without asking questions or making statements that you must see my nephew cannot answer.'

She was a little flushed as she turned to him. 'All right,' she said. 'If you'll listen. If you'll both listen,' she added, and looked back at Antony again.

There was nothing he wished less to do. 'I'll listen,' he assured her, 'but – '

'Don't say anything. Not yet.' She paused, arranging her thoughts. 'I know . . . I understand that when you accept a brief you're not bound to do anything but follow the solicitor's instructions. But sometimes you've been able to do more. You've been able to – '

'Meddle,' said Sir Nicholas succinctly, closing his mouth on the word with something like a snap.

' – to find out what really happened.' A touch of doggedness had crept into Eleanor's tone. 'That's what I want you to do this time, Mr. Maitland. Because, you see, Malcolm didn't do anything wrong.'

'Wait a bit!' He didn't really like being reminded of the publicity that had sometimes attended his affairs, but having gone so far he'd have to hear her out. 'Are you telling me you know this, of your own knowledge?'

'I *know*.' She was desperately in earnest. 'He wouldn't do a thing like that.'

If there had been anything wanting to complete Maitland's disenchantment it was that. A simple statement that he had heard, he felt, a hundred times before, and usually without any basis in fact. 'I'm afraid that wouldn't carry much weight in court,' he told her, with calculated brutality.

'I know that, but – '

'Besides, Miss Wyatt, it's something no one can know, even about their nearest and dearest. There's no end to – to the folly,' he said, choosing this time the kindest word, 'of which human beings are capable.'

41

'I know I've no right to speak for him. No right at all,' She chose for argument what was, perhaps, for her, the most difficult part of his remarks. 'Only I hoped Mary would come to you, but when I asked her yesterday – '

'I am becoming confused,' Sir Nicholas complained. Eleanor was both indignant and inclined to be tearful, and Antony was glad enough to turn from her and give his attention to his uncle. He was, in fact, grateful for the intervention, which might or might not have been purposely arranged to give their visitor a breathing space.

'Malcolm is Malcolm Harte, my client,' he said. 'And Mary, if I'm not mistaken, is Mary Reynolds, who is engaged to be married to him.'

'Not any more!' said Eleanor. 'She was quite horrid about it. Said she wouldn't dream of interfering with the course of justice . . . as if it's justice to have someone found guilty who isn't.'

'And she has broken the engagement?'

'Yes, she has.'

'I see. But however sympathetic we may feel, Miss Wyatt, there is still the little matter of proof.'

'I thought you understood. That's what I want you to find.'

'That's rather a tall order.' The conversation seemed to be going round in circles. She was so much in earnest, and he despaired of ever making her see . . . 'Look here, I'm going to do my best for him, you know.'

'I'm sure of that.' She spoke quickly, afraid of offending him, but she wasn't really convinced. 'I know I'm asking a lot, but if you knew Malcolm – '

'I've met him.'

'Yes, but . . . just once, I suppose, in prison.'

'That's true. Do you know him well, Miss Wyatt?'

The flush was back; she probably regarded it as an affliction, but in fact it was rather attractive. 'Not as well as I should like,' she said firmly. 'But well enough to know – '

'Not that again!' said Antony.

She didn't pretend to misunderstand him. 'You can laugh if you like,' she said, with only a little resentment in her tone. He had thought he spoke dead seriously, but perhaps his eyes betrayed his amusement. 'What did you think of him yourself then?'

That wasn't an easy question. 'A likeable chap,' said Antony, going warily. And he was lying to me, or at least not telling all the truth, but it wouldn't do to tell her that. 'I have really had very little opportunity to judge.'

'Then don't you think you should give yourself that opportunity?' He admired the quickness of that, she was less nervous now, but it didn't make things any easier.

'As you said, Miss Wyatt, I work to my brief. My instructions are that Harte is innocent – '

'But you don't believe it.'

For the second time Sir Nicholas intervened. 'You are raising matters again, my dear, upon which it would be quite improper for my nephew to comment.'

'Yes, but . . . if I can't convince him – ' She broke off there, looking helplessly from one of them to the other. Sir Nicholas, who seemed to have endless patience this evening, said gently,

'We can at least discuss your reasons for thinking that your friend has done nothing wrong.'

She thought about that for a moment, her nervousness returning now that she had been brought face to face with the purpose of her visit, without possibility of further evasion. 'Well, first of all there's Malcolm's character, but you say that doesn't count.'

'If you can tell us anything specific – '

'He's frightfully honest, I know there's nothing

43

specially creditable about that, but when someone is terribly careful about not getting too much change . . . things like that . . . you don't expect them to plan a jewel robbery. Then he's always seemed to me a very gentle person – '

'Who could under no circumstances commit a murder?' said Antony, feeling that he had been out of the conversation for long enough. As he spoke he was suddenly conscious of the pain in his shoulder; a nagging pain that was always there, ever since the wartime injury that caused it, but that he was more inclined to notice when, as now, he was tired.

That brought another silence. 'No,' said Eleanor doubtfully at last. 'I don't think I could say that. But not that way.'

'The prosecution's case will be that it was a spur of the moment killing, done "that way" because the lump of amethyst was the only weapon to hand.'

'But if he didn't commit the theft – '

'We're arguing in circles again. Go on with your analysis of Harte's character.'

'I'm not really competent, but I'll tell you one thing I'm sure of. If he had done it – both things, the theft and the murder – he wouldn't have denied it when he was caught. He wouldn't be lying to his solicitor, and to you, and presently to the court under oath.'

'Now you do interest me, Miss Wyatt. Can you tell me something about his religious convictions?'

'Nothing really, except that I know he goes to church, and I think he's an R.C. But anybody who believed at all wouldn't take an oath on the Bible, would they, and then tell lies?'

'I'm sorry to disillusion you, but it has been known.'

'Not if they really believed,' said Eleanor stubbornly. 'Anyway, you could ask Malcolm, couldn't you?'

'I could, of course.' Now what was he getting into?

He glanced at Sir Nicholas, whose rather austere expression told him nothing. 'How long have you known Harte, Miss Wyatt?'

'Since last March. Only three months really, because of course I haven't seen him since he was arrested. But that's long enough to know . . . well, some things, isn't it?'

'That depends upon the degree of your intimacy.'

'I suppose I saw him once or twice a week all that time.'

'How did that come about?'

'Because Mary and I are friends, though I never knew she could be so hard-hearted and – and self-righteous. We were at school together, and that's why I thought Malcolm might be a Catholic, because Mary is. I'm not. Anyway, we kept on being friends after we left the convent and we both became engaged at almost exactly the same time last March. So, of course, we got together, the four of us, to celebrate. And after that we all got on so well that we just kept on meeting.'

'You yourself are engaged to be married then,' said Sir Nicholas.

'Yes.' For a moment Antony thought she wasn't going to say anything more, but then she added in something of a rush, 'To Laurence Blake, he's a crime reporter for the *Courier*.'

'I've seen his by-line,' Antony told her. 'What does he think about all this?'

'He thinks I'm . . . making a fool of myself,' said Eleanor. 'He said – '

'Having gone so far, I think you had better tell us what he said,' said Sir Nicholas, after a moment.

'He said he wouldn't want to have anything more to do with someone who had so little self-respect,' said Eleanor, looking now at her hands.

'But still you came here?'

'I had to, didn't I? I mean, if I felt it was right – '

'Yes, I see.' Antony glanced at his uncle, but there was still nothing to be told from the older man's face. He would like to have said, 'That was brave of you,' but it might sound condescending. Instead he attempted to bring the conversation back to the point again. 'Have you any other reason for thinking Harte innocent, besides what you have told us of his character?'

'Well, I do know . . . somebody's telling a lie.'

'Now there you do interest me.' Something he could use, perhaps, without necessarily following her example of implicit belief.

'It's a very small point,' said Eleanor, unwilling now to display the poverty of her wares.

'Tell us.'

'Only that Sarah – Lady Bowling – said she saw Malcolm going downstairs, after we had all gone to our rooms, you know.'

'And you think she didn't see him? It's a small point, because he admits – '

'Yes, I know that. But she told us, and I expect she told the police too, that she was on her way to the bathroom, and I saw her halfway down the stairs. She was standing quite still, and if she saw Malcolm it must have been then.'

'How did you come to see her, Miss Wyatt?'

'I remembered I had mother's sleeping pills in my handbag, she'd forgotten them, and asked me to bring them for her at the last minute. I was in the east wing, where Sarah and Sir Leonard were, and Mother and Daddy were in the west; so I had to cross the main landing, past the head of the stairs, to get from one to the other.'

'Where was Harte sleeping?'

'In the west wing.'

'In that case it seems unlikely that Lady Bowling

could have seen him as she said. I imagine each wing has its own bathroom.'

'There were two in the east wing, and I dare say two in the other, I don't know.'

'So it would have been impossible for her to see Harte without emerging on to the main landing. I knew that plan would come in useful,' added Antony in parenthesis to his uncle, who only looked blank, not having been in court that day. 'But it is, as you said, Miss Wyatt, a very small point.'

'She was standing very still, I thought she didn't want anybody to see her,' said Eleanor.

'Did you think that at the time, or did it occur to you later?'

'Well . . . not till later, I suppose,' she said reluctantly. 'All the same – '

'Are you suggesting that Lady Bowling might have killed George DeLisle?'

'No, I . . . I just thought it might give you a starting point, that's all.'

'Always supposing I want one,' Antony said. But he was thinking, inevitably, suppose, after all, she's right about Harte's character. I ought at least to make a little more certain, because the prospect of prison for an innocent man . . . he shook off that thought, which he found oppressive, and looked at his uncle. Sir Nicholas had been unusually forbearing that evening, at least since they had come downstairs; obviously he had taken a fancy to Eleanor Wyatt, but that didn't mean he was going to condone any 'meddling'. In fact, that was probably why he had insisted on sharing the interview, to prevent just what seemed to be happening now. All the same . . . 'I can't promise anything,' he said, turning back to the girl. 'I've an idea that could settle things, one way or the other. But you may not like what I find out, you know.'

'You're going to help us,' said Eleanor eagerly.

'I may not be able to, you must understand that.' I may not want to, but no need to be quite so specific.

'Will you need me as a witness?'

'I can't say for sure, but I shouldn't think so.' He smiled at her. 'I don't think much of your "evidence", you know. Unless you can tell me anything new about that evening. Perhaps, while you're here, we could go over that. The clearer I have it in my own mind . . . '

Half an hour later, after he had seen Eleanor Wyatt out, he went back to the study to find Sir Nicholas on his feet. 'I wouldn't have believed it if I hadn't seen it with my own eyes,' said Sir Nicholas coldly. 'That's a nice girl, Antony, and you've no right to encourage her in her foolishness.'

'I told her quite plainly, Uncle Nick – '

'So you did, but do you think she listened to you? She's gone home grateful, thinking you can do something to help her.'

'I said I had an idea, and that's perfectly true.'

'What sort of an idea? I warned you, Antony – '

'Yes, but this has nothing to do with what may happen in court. I thought,' said Antony, holding the door and allowing his uncle to precede him into the hall, 'that it might be a good idea if I went to see Father William.'

Sir Nicholas, who had reached the staircase, clutched at the newel post with a dramatic gesture, as though he needed its support. 'Anything that entails your getting in touch again with that old sinner – '

'He's a good friend of mine,' said Maitland, amused. 'Besides, it was you, if you remember, who defended him when he needed it.'

Sir Nicholas did not like the reminder, and said so. He was not even appeased by the discovery that there was some brandy left, after all. But he did not forget to ask his nephew what the idea was, and how William Webster could help him. Antony was ready enough to explain, but already he could see the difficulties ahead, and did not attempt to argue when Sir Nicholas pointed them out to him.

FRIDAY, the second day

The first witness the following morning was the DeLisles' butler, a man named Canning. Maitland, whose views on the whole race of menservants were soured by his acquaintance with Gibbs, eyed him curiously as he went into the box. A tall man with a grave look about him, a manner that was bland but by no means obsequious. Garfield wanted one thing from him, and one thing only. An account of how he had carefully locked up the house on the night of the crime.

'You say, Mr. Canning, that you personally checked the doors. Did you do the same for the windows?'

'Certainly I did.'

'It was a warm night, was it not, when some of them might very likely have been left open?'

'That is true. But Mrs. DeLisle was very particular . . . a nervous lady,' said the witness indulgently. 'I mean, of course, she is very particular, always, but that night she mentioned it to me again, though it wasn't really necessary, because of the jewellery being in the house, I suppose. I personally checked all the downstairs windows at ten o'clock, except for the lounge windows, which of course had to be left until the gentlemen had retired.'

'What time was that?'

'Almost exactly eleven-thirty.'

'The morning-room window that was found open the next day – '

'Was certainly closed and the catch secured by ten o'clock.'

Nothing much there for the defence. Maitland, who had intended to let the witness go without questioning him, found himself on his feet. A promise was a promise, after all, even though he had also implied to Uncle Nick that it would make no difference to his handling of the case in court.

'This catch on the window, Mr. Canning. Is it burglar-proof, by any chance?'

'Oh, no, I shouldn't think so. But there were no marks to indicate a forcible entry. The detective said so, and I saw with my own eyes – '

'Thank you, Mr. Canning.' Garfield, who had started to come to his feet, sat down again. He was quite right, of course, this had all been gone into at length with one of the police witnesses yesterday; but no harm, in view of his new resolve, in taking a leaf out of Counsel for the Prosecution's book and emphasising the point a little. 'Just one more point. What time was it when you checked the window in the drawing-room?'

'At eleven-thirty, sir, or not more than a minute after that. Immediately upon the gentlemen retiring.'

'Did you see or hear anything while you were in the hall on that occasion?'

'Nothing at all.'

'Or earlier, when you were clearing up in the dining-room, for instance?'

'That was done promptly, and all finished by about ten past ten. At that time, I believe, the entire party were in the lounge.'

'And later, when Mr. Henry DeLisle rang for the decanters?'

'I took the tray in at about twenty to eleven. As I crossed the hall I did get the impression that the study door had just closed, but I cannot say who had gone in. I saw nobody else.'

'Nor heard anybody?'

The witness wrinkled his brow. 'That is more difficult, sir. There could have been a step on the stairs, but when I glanced that way there was nobody in sight, and of course it wasn't my business to question the goings and comings of our guests.'

'Nor is it our business to enquire into them,' said Garfield at his coldest. 'Your lordship will agree – '

'There might be two opinions about that, but I have finished with the witness,' said Maitland quickly. 'Thank you, Mr. Canning.'

Mr. Justice Conroy gave him a suspicious look, but refrained from comment. 'Do you wish to re-examine the witness, Mr. Garfield?' he enquired.

'One question, my lord, to clarify the matter.' But there was nothing fresh to ask the witness, only a repetition . . .

The third juror, a stout, benevolent-looking woman who prided herself on her business acumen, didn't like Mr. Canning. The world would be a better place if there weren't men like him, ready to sell their services for money. It would do that stuck-up DeLisle man good to have to polish his own silver for a change, answer his own doorbell. It was almost enough to make you sympathetic towards the defence, almost but not quite. Harte was an underdog, true, but even worse than the witness, letting his employers put upon him, impose on his free time; if most fellows like him didn't stand up for themselves, the world would be a sorry place. And when she said, 'stand up for themselves' she didn't mean theft and murder. She hadn't made up her mind yet, of course, hear all the evidence first. But Counsel for the Prosecution had been convincing, very.

Of course, the other one still had to have his say. She wondered idly whether he really believed his client was innocent.
Lawyers were such hypocrites, as far as she could judge. She
mistrusted a man with that humorous look about him, probably
tiresomely frivolous. And there wasn't rhyme nor reason to be
made of his questions so far.

It was to be hoped the trial didn't last long. John couldn't be
trusted to keep the business on an even keel, a pushover for any
wildcat scheme. Well, she'd warned him, but take your eyes off
that man for a couple of days and anything might happen.
Didn't seem able to realise, either, that they couldn't afford a
big inventory. Still a week – it wasn't likely to be more than a
week, was it? – should be all right.

She wasn't impressed with her fellow-jurors. The foreman
now, they'd have done better with her to guide them; made up
their own minds already, like as not, no more sense than to
believe all they heard. Now she, well yes, she was inclined to
believe the prosecution, but it was an intellectual assent to what
she had heard, not based on emotionalism as was most probably
the case with the others. The other women jurors most likely felt
motherly towards the prisoner, thought he could do with feeding
up, no more sense than to be taken in by a good-looking face.
Well, she'd speak her mind when the time came.

You had to hand it to him, he'd acted with decision for once
in his life, but then had no more sense than to get caught. A
weakling, a born loser. Now, if she were to take to crime, which
of course she wouldn't. She smiled at the thought and Maitland,
who happened to be looking her way, wondered vaguely what
she had found in the evidence to amuse her. But if she did, it
wouldn't end like this. She'd back her own brains against the
police any day, though of course it was more likely they'd never
even know anything was wrong. The perfect crime. A pity, perhaps, that there was no occasion for it. If you kept your wits
about you – not like some people she could name – things would
go your way all right. A clear profit at the end of the year, that
was all she asked, and if John hadn't the sense to see how it was

52

to be obtained, she had. And no need to worry about her fellow-jurors; a dull lot they might be, but they'd see sense all right when she put it to them where their duty lay. No squeamishness. But, of course, you had to hear all the evidence, she hadn't made up her mind yet . . .

The next witness had already been sworn. This was Grace DeLisle, a pleasant-faced, grey-haired woman who had retained a good figure into middle age, but who had no pretensions to smartness. It was evident from the start that Garfield approved of her, his natural stiffness of manner abated a trifle so that he looked almost genial.

'What I want you to tell us, Mrs. DeLisle, is how the accused came to be included in the weekend party at your house, the thirteenth to the fourteenth of June last.'

She had none of her husband's self-assurance. 'Yes, well, I thought – '

'There is no hurry, madam. Just tell us in your own words,' Garfield encouraged her, when it became apparent that she wasn't going to finish the sentence.

'I don't quite know . . . it was all so simple, really. I knew they were engaged, Malcolm and Mary, I mean, so I thought it would be nice if they could have a little time together. Because Mary lives at home, with lots of brothers and sisters, and Malcolm was in lodgings where, of course, he couldn't take her. I mean, even today there are some things – ' She broke off again, looking helpless.

It was evident that Garfield had not yet got what he wanted. His air of patient courtesy became a little strained, but not really sufficiently so to fluster the witness further. 'You are speaking of Malcolm Harte, the accused, and Mary Reynolds, your husband's secretary, are you not?' he enquired.

53

'Oh, yes, of course.'

'Let us go about it more slowly. When did your husband first ask you to issue invitations for that weekend?'

'It wasn't really Henry . . . I mean, George told us at dinner on the Tuesday night, the Tuesday before – '

'Tuesday, the ninth of June?'

'The Tuesday before,' said the witness, declining to commit herself. 'George told us at dinner that he had arranged for the Bowlings to see the jewellery on Saturday evening, and would I get in touch with Lady Bowling to make the invitation official. Then Henry said it would be nice to make it something of an occasion, so why not ask some other people as well, and I said it was short notice.'

'But you managed, in spite of that, to get together quite a number of people.'

'Yes. Henry said they'd come – like a shot, he said – if I told them about the jewellery, and of course a lot of people are interested in it. We owed the Wyatts hospitality, so that was easily decided, and asking Eleanor we had to ask Laurence Blake as well, because he's her fiancé. And when I spoke to Eleanor she said she wished Godfrey could see the jewellery because he's crazy about old-fashioned settings; and that would make us an even number, of course, though I'd rather have had another woman because of George, you know, so I asked him and he said he'd love to come.'

'Godfrey is – ?'

'Godfrey Thurlow. Eleanor works for him at the Sefton Gallery.'

'Thank you, Mrs. DeLisle.' This was going the long way round, though Maitland found it interesting. 'Now we come to the invitation to the accused.'

'Poor Malcolm,' said the witness, sighing. 'I shouldn't say that, I know, but it does seem so sad.'

'The invitation, madam.'

'Oh, dear, yes, I was going to tell you, wasn't I? I went up to town on Wednesday, and called in at the shop after lunch. Malcolm asked me if it would be convenient if he brought the jewellery immediately after lunch on the Saturday – and I knew it was no good asking him for that meal because the shop stays open until one – then he could come straight from work; and he said he'd bring Mary with him, then they could have a walk on the common afterwards if it was fine. So I asked him when the wedding was and he said in a month's time, and it couldn't come too quickly for him because it was so difficult finding places to go without spending a lot of money they couldn't afford. And I thought, well! If George and Henry could wish a week-end party on me at short notice I could add a guest or two myself, and perhaps Henry wouldn't mind so very much having them there in a crowd. So I asked Malcolm, and he said he'd love to stay over if Mary could, and when I found her she said yes without any hesitation, so that was arranged. Henry did say it wasn't really necessary when I told him, but I think he saw my point about the crowd and didn't carry on about it.'

It was queer, wasn't it, how the most nervous witnesses often became the most talkative. Garfield had made no attempt to stem the flood, but to Maitland's eye at least his earlier approbation had turned a little sour. 'Am I correct in saying then, Mrs. DeLisle, that it was in consequence of a conversation with the accused that you issued the invitation to him for the weekend of the thirteenth June?'

'Yes, but – '

'What he said aroused your sympathy?'

'Oh, yes!'

'Thank you, Mrs. DeLisle, that is all.'

She had turned to leave the box when the judge

voice stopped her. 'One moment, madam. The defence has some questions for you, I believe.'

'Thank you, my lord.' Maitland was on his feet. 'Mrs. DeLisle, you have told us very clearly how your guest list came to be made up. Can you tell me by what date the invitations had all been issued and accepted?'

'It all had to be done by telephone,' said the witness apologetically, as though counsel was likely to censure her for this casual way of doing things. 'I spoke to Lady Bowling on Wednesday morning before I went out, but of course the arrangement had really been made already. Then to William and Rose Wyatt after I got home in the afternoon, and it turned out they know the Bowlings quite well, so everything was working out most satisfactorily.'

'And earlier in the afternoon you had spoken to Malcolm Harte and Mary Reynolds?'

'Oh, yes, I told . . . but perhaps you weren't listening.'

Maitland smiled at her. 'I was listening, madam. I'm afraid I have to ask you to be patient with a certain amount of repetition. That is the majority of your guests accounted for. The others?'

'I spoke to Eleanor at the Gallery on Thursday morning, and directly after that to Godfrey Thurlow. Then I rang Laurence Blake straight away, but it wasn't until the afternoon that I managed to speak to him.'

'And they all accepted your invitation? Mr. Thurlow's at least had been almost asked for, hadn't it?'

'Oh, no! At least, I didn't see it that way.'

'But surely, Mrs. DeLisle, it was as much a consequence of your conversation with Miss Eleanor Wyatt as your invitation to my client was of your conversation with him.'

'Yes, of course, but I don't think either of them . . . '

This was a tedious business. The fourth juror was younger than her neighbour, and slimmer; an attractive young woman with something of a roving eye. She had chosen her place carefully as the line of jurors moved into court; it was a pity about the old cow on her right, of course, but on her left was by far the most handsome man on the jury, and she had seen from the look he gave her that he was by no means impervious to her own charms. Wouldn't be surprised if he was a film actor.

How long would the trial take, anyway? It all seemed cut and dried, and the fun wouldn't start until they got into the jury room. She'd bet they wouldn't get out of it again before she'd got something fixed up with Handsome on her left. Not that he was by any means the only pebble on the beach in the courtroom. But the only one she had any chance of, worse luck.

She had already summed up the chief figures in the drama. The judge, who had a cherubic cast of countenance, might have been fun in his younger days. Counsel for the Prosecution, though not nearly so old, was still well beyond her usual range. Attractive, though, in a frightening kind of way. Cold. She didn't think you could say that about the other one, Maitland, the judge called him. Could be fun, she wouldn't mind half an hour alone with him. Or the one sitting next to him, who had had even less to say. Clever men, she supposed, all of them; perhaps too clever for comfort.

But the one she'd really like a chance with was the prisoner. The word 'insignificant' never occurred to her; he was good-looking enough to be presentable, which was important in its way, but more than that he was of a type she had had some experience with and considered made the best lovers. And he was afraid. If she knew anything about men, that was true, and she found it fascinating. It was no wonder, either. That opening speech the prosecuting counsel had made was enough to scare anyone. It would be interesting to see what the defence had to say, she hoped it was something good. As to character, she thought the accused just the kind to break out suddenly into violence. Repressed. But it would more likely be passion than

57

gain that moved him. That was what she thought, anyway, and they'd have a job changing her mind.

In the meantime, she wished she was a thousand miles from here. Well, not so much as a thousand, perhaps, in her own comfortable house with Bill mixing the drinks and dinner to be sent round from a nearby restaurant. And afterwards . . . Bill was staid . . . Bill was stolid . . . Bill was familiar country and she needed a change. But Bill was safe. And even under the present arrangement there were opportunities. When she wasn't stuck in court, listening . . .

Counsel for the Defence had finished now, Garfield was on his feet again. 'One last question, Mrs. DeLisle. Had you any intention of asking the prisoner to spend the weekend at your home before you talked with him on Wednesday, the tenth June?'

'No, it hadn't occurred to me until then.'

'Thank you, madam. That is all.' As Garfield seated himself again Maitland glanced his way. Well, he had cause enough for self-satisfaction. All that probing on the part of the defence, and nothing to show for it. And any small effect it might have had on the collective mind of the jury destroyed in one brief sentence. Uncle Nick had warned him, of course, but did that make it any more palatable? He came out of his reverie to hear the judge announcing the luncheon adjournment; rather early for that, meant most likely that the old boy wanted to get away early this afternoon. Which was all the better for his own plans.

Geoffrey Horton was in excellent spirits. 'That was more like it,' he said, almost before they had seated themselves. Antony gave him a sour look.

'What do you mean?' he asked.

'You know perfectly well what I mean,' said Geoffrey, who hadn't known Maitland for nearly eighteen years for nothing. 'Something's happened to change your mind.'

'I have been told,' said Antony, with a grin that anybody could have seen was completely mirthless, 'that our client wouldn't do a thing like that.'

Derek Stringer said, 'Good God!' placidly, and then turned to give instructions to the waiter, because he could see that neither of his companions was in a mood to attend to that just then. For himself, he had given up being surprised at anything Maitland might do or say years ago.

Horton, however, seemed a little daunted. 'I wish you'd explain,' he complained.

'There's very little to tell you. Eleanor Wyatt came to see me last night – '

'The Wyatt girl? Does she know anything?'

'One small, insignificant fact. Lady Bowling could not have seen Harte going downstairs on her way to the bathroom, as she has claimed. She would have had to come out on to the main landing. That can be proved, I imagine, from the plan; but Miss Wyatt says that she saw Lady Bowling standing very still, halfway down the stairs.'

'What time was that?'

'She thinks about ten minutes after she went to bed. That would be ten-forty, more or less, which ties in with what Lady Bowling says.'

'I don't see that that proves anything, one way or the other.' Geoffrey's spirits were mercurial today; he was now as cast down as he had been euphoric before.

'Of course it doesn't.'

'Then – '

'He doesn't want to disoblige the lady,' said Derek. The waiter was weaving his way towards the bar.

'It isn't that.' But no need to explain, Derek was only trying to get a rise out of him. Besides, it wasn't easy . . .

I'm not omniscient, the girl may be right and I wrong, and if that is the case . . . 'The thing is, I had an idea.'

'What sort of an idea?' asked Geoffrey, suspicious now.

'I thought I'd go and see Father William. With his connections he ought to be able to tell me for sure who stole the jewellery, and if it wasn't Harte – '

'Who,' asked Stringer, 'is Father William?'

'A jeweller of my acquaintance,' said Antony, but Geoffrey put it more bluntly.

'A fence,' he said.

FRIDAY, the second day (continued)

When the court reconvened, the prosecution were ready to call Mary Reynolds. Remembering his talk with Eleanor, Maitland watched the girl with interest as she took the oath on a Douai bible, and answered Garfield's preliminary questions. She was, he estimated, about five foot four; a pretty mouse of a girl, but appealing enough in her way, and with a soft, pleasant voice. From her he glanced at the prisoner, and saw him more alert than he had appeared during the morning session, his eyes fixed on the witness with rather painful intensity. Not for the first time, he regretted that he had not spent more time on his interview with his client. The Lord Chancellor's resolve,

> *I'll never assume that a rogue or a thief*
> *Is a gentleman worthy implicit belief,*
> *Because his attorney has sent me a brief,*

might be a good one, but the converse could hold true as well. He had been guilty of judging his client, which wasn't his job; that could and would be remedied, however. What he was wondering now was whether Malcolm Harte had any idea of the change of attitude on the part of his betrothed. That is, if Eleanor Wyatt was right, and she had sounded very sure. Or perhaps she had spoken in a misguided attempt to enlist his sympathy. It never occurred to him that the plan – if it had been a plan – might, in part, have succeeded.

'Now, Miss Reynolds – ' Garfield's tone was almost fatherly, which sent Maitland's mind – for the moment undisciplined – off on another tack. His opponent had three children, as far as he remembered, who must be in their teens by now. How did Garfield rate as a father? Was he unexpectedly indulgent, or as severe as you would assume from his attitude to the world at large. And if . . . at this point Stringer nudged him, and he brought his thoughts back to the courtroom in a hurry.

'. . . I want to ask you about the invitation you received to spend the night of the thirteenth June last at the DeLisles' home,' Garfield was saying. 'Mrs. DeLisle spoke to you on the afternoon of Wednesday, the tenth, did she not?'

Was it worth while exacerbating the prosecution by protesting at this blatant, but harmless, leading of the witness? On the whole, he thought not. 'Yes,' said Mary, and this time had to be asked to speak up. When she had repeated her answer, and did not seem inclined to say any more, Garfield said encouragingly:

'There was some conversation between you on that occasion, I am sure.'

'Only that she said she thought it would be nice if Malcolm and I spent the weekend with them. I gathered that Malcolm had already agreed, so of course I did so too.'

'And you went out to Wimbledon together after you had closed the shop on the Saturday?'

'That's right.'

'Tell me, Miss Reynolds, after your conversation with Mrs. DeLisle, after she had left the shop, did you also have some conversation with the accused about the weekend invitation.'

'Yes, he came back to the office to talk to me.'

'You were alone together?'

'We were.' But her voice was down to a whisper again, and for the second time she had to be asked to speak more loudly. 'We were,' she repeated, and this time glanced for a moment at Malcolm Harte, and then quickly away again.

'I must ask you to tell us the substance of that conversation, Miss Reynolds.'

'Yes, I . . . he said it would make a nice change, wouldn't it? And I said, yes, but all those people! And he said, never mind, it was better than nothing.'

'And then?'

'He said – ' She hesitated again, but this time her voice was quite clear and firm when she went on. 'He said, Don't tell me you don't want to go, I had to practically ask for the invitation.'

There was a stir in the courtroom at that. Garfield allowed the silence between him and his witness to lengthen, letting what had been said sink in. Maitland glanced at his client and saw that Harte had his head bent now, not looking any longer at the girl in the witness box. Then Garfield said, still fatherly, pleased with himself and her, 'There is just one other matter, Miss Reynolds. You are engaged to be married to the prisoner, are you not?'

That brought another almost silent answer, but again when she had to repeat her words she did so clearly. 'I was . . . at that time. I don't consider myself engaged to him now.' The prisoner's head was still bent; he seemed to be contemplating his hands.

'I am sure we all understand your feelings. But – at that time – the date of your wedding was fixed, I believe.'

'We were going to be married on the eleventh of July – that was a Saturday, too.'

'And had you made any plans for your honeymoon?'

'Yes, we were going to the Continent.'

'Let me digress for a moment. Did you hear, from the prisoner or from any other person, that these plans might have to be changed?'

'No.' She looked and sounded puzzled and Garfield added, as though to enlighten her,

'At Mr. George DeLisle's insistence.'

'But it was all fixed. I don't think he would have done that.'

That brought Maitland halfway to his feet, but Garfield had proceeded smoothly to his next point and he subsided again with his objection unformulated.

'Your plans were fixed, and you were going to the Continent,' Garfield was saying.

'Yes, we were flying to Paris, and then hiring a Volkswagen and touring for a couple of weeks.'

'Was this your idea or the prisoner's?'

'Malcolm's. He was very keen, so I thought we might as well.'

'And had any specific destination been mentioned?'

'He thought we might finish up in Amsterdam, and come home from there. You can arrange to leave hire cars – '

'Yes, precisely. Amsterdam,' said Garfield, underlining his point. 'I wonder if you can tell us, Miss Reynolds . . . had the prisoner ever discussed his financial position with you?'

'Only in the most general terms.' She hesitated, and then added, as Garfield made no move to prompt her, 'I knew he was hard up, of course.'

'And yet he suggested this expensive holiday. And now, Miss Reynolds,' said Garfield, carefully leaving the witness no time to qualify his statement, 'let us recapitulate a little . . . '

The fifth juror, who wasn't a film star after all but a clerk in a shipping office, thought that on the whole the prisoner had poor taste. A girl like this one, not much fun, and not even reliable when the chips were down. A lie would have cost so little, and all that stuff about swearing on a different bible, it made him tired.

Mum and Dad would have said it mattered, of course. Thou shalt not take the name of the Lord thy God in vain, *he remembered that from the old days. Probably someone had filled this girl up with all that nonsense, and she hadn't the sense to see what crap it all was. He'd been in a tight corner or two himself, and where would telling the truth get you? Just deeper into the mire.*

Last Friday, for instance. Who'd have thought old Tomlinson would come back to the office again in the afternoon, when everyone knew he always left for the country straight after lunch. His own lunch had been a protracted one, an unforgivable breach of office discipline about which he'd been warned a couple of times already. 'You're not indispensable, you know,' Tomlinson had said the last time, sneering, only too glad to get something on him if the truth were known, an old chap like him, past his best. But it would have been awkward just now to get the sack, with no savings and work hard to find. Might have had to go back home for a bit, listen to a few sermons, and that wouldn't suit his book, not now or any time.

So he'd thought quickly. He'd met Mr. Saville . . . well, that bit was true enough, a respected client, not one old Tomlinson would want to offend, or would countenance his staff offending, if it came to that. And Mr. Saville had kept him talking, nothing to be done about that, on and on he'd talked. Well, it hadn't been strictly true, not true at all if you came right down to it. But the beauty of it was there was little or no chance of being found out. Because what Saville had told him, in the few minutes they were together, was that he was going into hospital for a serious operation. And by the time he was about again there wasn't much chance of his ever comparing notes with Tomlinson. Not that it would matter by that time. He'd have saved something, be able to laugh it off.

Of course, even Mum and Dad would admit there was a difference between lying and swearing to a lie. Not that they approved of either. That was all in the past, though, he wouldn't hesitate himself if ever it came to the point. Those old stories were for children, not for grown men. This girl, Mary Reynolds, hadn't grown up, that was what was wrong with her. He'd swear the lass next to him wouldn't be so namby pamby. Before the case was over . . . not before the other jurors, of course, but outside the court there'd surely be a chance. He'd suggest a drink or a cup of coffee, according to the time of day, and go on from there.

The defendant had pleaded Not Guilty, and that was a laugh, according to the prosecution. And presently he'd take the stand and swear his innocence, and nobody be a penny the worse for it that he could see. Some of his fellow-jurors might even believe what the prisoner said, thinking he wouldn't dare to take the oath and then lie. Thou shalt not take the name of the Lord thy God in vain. *This little girl was one of the superstitious ones, one of the weak ones. Interesting to see what Counsel for the Defence, who was now getting slowly to his feet, would make of her . . .*

It was obvious from the beginning that she regarded him as an enemy. Maitland made a mental note of the fact, without having time to wonder why. 'I shall not keep you long, Miss Reynolds,' he told her, 'but there are a few points arising out of my friend's questions. For instance, you talked over your honeymoon plans with my client, didn't you?'

'Oh, yes.'

'Were you in any way reluctant to take a continental holiday?'

'No. I hadn't thought, but once he suggested it I was as keen as he was.'

'I see. Do you remember when the suggestion was first made?'

'A long time before, back in March when we became engaged.'

'And if, perhaps, Mr. Harte had changed his mind after that he would have risked disappointing you.'

'Yes, I suppose so.'

'But it would not, after all, have been so very expensive a vacation.'

'No, we had it all planned out. It wouldn't have cost much more than staying in a big hotel in one of the resorts at home.'

'Not so extravagant, then?' He smiled at her, trying to establish some rapport, but she avoided his eye and answered primly.

'I wouldn't have agreed to it if I thought it would be extravagant.'

So far, so good. But his next question misfired badly. 'And when you say Mr. Harte was "hard up", Miss Reynolds − ?' he said, making the words a question. And she answered unhesitatingly,

'I knew he was worried about something. It *may* not have been that.'

That was pretty devastating. Try to retrieve the situation? Better not. 'Why did you think my client desired an invitation to the DeLisles' home?'

'Well, I − '

'Come, Miss Reynolds, there is no need to be shy about it. You were, after all, engaged to be married to him. You thought, very naturally, that he wanted the opportunity of being with you.'

'Yes, I did, but – '

'A perfectly normal explanation, nothing very sinister about it at all.'

'N-no.'

'And something happened, did it not, that Saturday night of which we are speaking, to confirm that impression?'

'I don't know what you mean.' She had a stubborn look about her, and probably the feeling in the court ran in her favour, but he couldn't let her get away with that. On this point at least the prisoner had been frank with him. 'I mean, Miss Reynolds, that you saw Mr. Harte again after the party had broken up for the night.'

He was quite reprehensibly glad to see that the statement shook her. She flushed scarlet, which in his experience was a very rare phenomenon indeed, and said, again almost inaudibly, 'Yes.'

'How did that come about?'

'He came to my room.'

'I am sorry, Miss Reynolds, I must ask you to repeat that. I doubt if his lordship can hear you, and the jury – '

'He came to my room. It wasn't what you're thinking – '

'I assure you, my mind is a blank upon the subject. I am waiting for you to enlighten me.'

'I mean, he knew I wouldn't,' said Mary, floundering badly. 'He said, "It wasn't quite what I expected, I wanted the chance to be alone with you." But, of course, I knew he shouldn't be there, I wouldn't let him stay.'

'Still, you did see him, and you can tell us at what time this interview took place.'

'I can, because I thought someone might notice him leaving my room, and I looked at my watch when he left and it wasn't so very late really. Not quite eleven.'

'After he had been downstairs to the study then,' said Maitland, turning a little so that the remark had the effect of being addressed to the jury. 'If we are to believe what my learned friend for the prosecution tells us, Miss Reynolds, Malcolm Harte had just robbed his employers and committed in the process a particularly brutal murder. Did you see any sign in his manner that either of these allegations was true?'

'N-no.' Again she sounded hesitant; this was obviously a new idea to her and she had to think about it. But even so she added, too quickly for Maitland to forestall her, 'But he did seem excited . . . well, elated, sort of.'

He tried again. 'But not as if – ' and this time she answered almost eagerly, before he could complete his question.

'I've never seen anybody who'd just committed a murder. I don't know.'

Garfield hardly needed to re-examine.

The next witness could scarcely have been more different. Whatever your standards, Maitland thought, Sarah Bowling was a beautiful woman. Her hair was a rich, dark red, dressed in some complicated fashion that he thought, in his innocence, must take hours of arrangement each morning; instead of being kept in place between visits to the hairdresser by liberal applications of spray – as Jenny could have told him, though she never used the stuff herself. Sarah had regular features, and the creamy pallor common in redheads. Her make-up was discreet, her manner quiet and deferential. Altogether, a sight for sore eyes, though Garfield, for some reason, seemed ill at ease with her. Surely it was the defence who had a right to be nervous . . . not a woman it would be easy to shake.

So she confirmed for Garfield her name, her address, her occupation. 'I suppose you would call me a house-wife,' she said with a delicious smile, so that even the judge – a man conscious of his own dignity – seemed tempted to smile in sympathy.

'Thank you, Lady Bowling,' said Garfield, un-amused. 'Now I must ask you to cast your mind back to the evening of the thirteenth of June last, which was a Saturday.'

'In view of what happened, that isn't difficult.'

'Will you tell us something of the events of that evening from, say, dinner time on.'

'There's very little to tell. Mrs. DeLisle is a charming hostess, and dinner passed very agreeably. Afterwards – I didn't notice the time myself, but my husband says it was about ten o'clock – Mr. George DeLisle brought some jewellery into the drawing-room to show us all. I was particularly interested because my husband had promised me . . . well, he promised to buy it for me "if the price was right". But the sketches were of even more interest, because the settings of the jewels themselves were so very old-fashioned. Mr. Henry DeLisle's draw-ings were really beautiful.'

'And after the viewing of the jewellery was over – ?'

'George DeLisle made his excuses, he said he had letters to write, and went away, taking the jewellery with him. I understand he went to his study. Almost immediately Mr. Thurlow and Laurence – Laurence Blake – left to go home, and Mr. Harte and the ladies of the party, including, of course, myself, went to bed.'

'It is what happened after that that we are particu-larly interested in, Lady Bowling.'

'This time I did notice what time it was. My watch said ten-forty, and it keeps very good time. I had occa-sion to leave my bedroom and I saw Mr. Harte going downstairs again.'

'My friend will ask you, I am sure, whether you are certain it was the accused that you saw.'

'Quite, quite certain.'

'Did he see you?'

'I think not.'

'And what happened then?'

'I went back to my room.'

'Thank you, Lady Bowling, that is very clear. Now, to retrace our steps a little . . . '

You had to admire a woman like that, soignée, imperturbable. The sixth juror would have been very glad to put herself in the same class, but she was realistic and only too aware of her own shortcomings. This Lady Bowling would know what she wanted, no squalid little triangles in her life. If the point came, she would cut the knot cleanly.

But who would have thought Sam would ever find out? After all these months, too, and it wasn't as if they hadn't been careful. Tuesday evenings, regular as clockwork, Sam would go to his Chess Club and the house would be free of his presence for four solid hours. He was a devotee, too, not likely to leave the play early for any reason. Until last night.

She could hear him now, explaining earnestly what had happened to bring him home, as though he were somehow to blame for the situation in which the three of them found themselves, as he was certainly to blame for the embarrassment. 'It was a match night, and Carpenter didn't turn up to play me, but no one else was free to give me a game.' And Jack, getting all cocky, as she might have expected, knowing him.

'Then you've only yourself to blame, haven't you? Not so much as knocking.' As if a man had the need to knock, in his own house.

At least, they hadn't been in bed. She had some decency, after all, and it was warm and comfortable on the couch, right in front of the fire. But it had been more difficult somehow, getting dressed, slipping shame-facedly into her dressing-gown, than it

70

would have been upstairs. Jack didn't seem to care, or if he did he didn't show it, but she was remembering that one time she and Sam . . . She'd tried talking to him then, 'Darling, it didn't mean anything,' but his answer had been inexplicable.

'That's the trouble, Tilly. Don't you understand? That's the trouble.'

It was funny, wasn't it, that there'd been no discussion, no recriminations? Only Jack, slipping into trousers and pullover, taking his coat almost jauntily from the rack in the hall, 'Be seeing you.' And Sam, turning away and going upstairs heavily into the spare room, where the bed wasn't even made up. She'd heard him at the linen cupboard, to and fro once or twice, as if he didn't quite know what was needed. He could have asked for help, couldn't he? Only somehow she hadn't quite liked to go up and offer it.

She wondered now whether he'd slept at all. She hadn't until almost morning, and then must have gone off deeply, she hadn't even heard him leave. But he'd gone all right, the spare room door ajar, the bed made up neatly. As though, she thought, with something like resentment, he couldn't bear to have me touch it. But he'd be home tonight, he hadn't taken anything with him, and perhaps she could talk to him; if only she could think of something to say, to break the barrier of silence. She didn't want to lose him. That was true.

If this Lady Bowling (the title suited her, she thought) had been caught in a similar situation she'd have known exactly what she wanted. But it was impossible to imagine her in circumstances over which she had no control. The prosecution must be nearing the end of their case now, they'd got it all. The motive, the opportunity, the fingerprints. Difficult to see what that chap for the defence could find to say, difficult to see how he could set about cross-examining anyone so self-assured as the witness . . .

Maitland wasn't too sure about that himself. Unless there were some real advantage to be gained, it was dangerous to stage an all out attack upon a witness. Dangerous in terms of loss of goodwill. And in this case, where Malcolm Harte admitted freely that he had gone down to the study at the time stated . . . all the same, if he were to get anywhere at all every slightest lead must be followed. He'd just have to chance it.

He started in a low key, by getting Sarah Bowling to repeat everything she had already said about the evening in question. Garfield had an impatient, scornful look, but there wasn't really much he could complain about except, perhaps, that the court's time was being wasted. 'Now, Lady Bowling,' said Maitland when she had finished, quite unperturbed by the repetition, 'you say the jewellery, or rather, the jewels that comprised it, was to be a gift to you from your husband.'

She smiled at him. 'If the price was right,' she said. And then, in unnecessary explanation, 'That's a quotation.'

Difficult not to respond to her friendliness. 'Was there any talk that evening about the price?'

'No, of course not. It was a private matter. I gathered that my husband had already been informed of it.'

'Do you think he would have accepted the offer?'

'Oh, I think so.' She was smiling again, but this time something about her expression disturbed him. As though she knew something that he didn't, some information that she had no intention of parting with. Well, that was probably true.

'I see,' he said. He was fumbling, and he knew it. He was conscious of Geoffrey, very intent behind him; and that Derek had caught up with the note and wanted to attract his attention. 'Was this gift to celebrate some special occasion, Lady Bowling?'

'An unbirthday present,' she said.

The judge looked up, and Garfield said without waiting for him to speak, 'I think the witness means, No, your lordship. Is that correct?'

'Quite correct. There was no special occasion for the gift.'

'I wonder, Lady Bowling – ' That was Maitland, taking up the thread of his questions. 'Has Sir Leonard repeated his offer?'

'I don't quite understand, I'm afraid.' For the first time he sensed some uneasiness in her manner; so that when Stringer, despairing of attracting his attention, pushed a note along the table in front of him, he ignored the scrawled words, 'LEAVE IT!' and pushed on eagerly.

'The jewels he wanted were stolen, but they are not the only – diamonds and emeralds, was it not? – in the world. Nor are DeLisle Brothers the only jewellers.'

'No, I see what you mean. We haven't spoken of the matter lately, but I dare say he was on the look out for what he wanted. I know what *I* wanted . . . the beautiful things that Henry DeLisle had sketched for me.'

'I see,' said Maitland again. It was a habit that Derek had remonstrated with him about from time to time, but you couldn't deny it was useful in filling a gap. 'Let us return to the evening of the thirteenth June, Lady Bowling. You have told my learned friend that after Mr. Thurlow and Mr. Blake left the house the party broke up, and everyone – with the exception of Mr. Henry DeLisle, your husband, and Mr. William Wyatt – retired for the night.'

'That's right. And, of course, George DeLisle was in the study, but I didn't know that at the time.'

'Thank you. We must on no account forget Mr. George DeLisle. Who started the move among the ladies to retire at ten-thirty?'

'Why, I . . . I don't remember.'

73

'I think perhaps if you make an effort – '

'My lord!' said Garfield, rising in a hurry. 'The witness has answered the question.'

'But perhaps not as fully as she is able, Mr. Garfield. I think we must allow Mr. Maitland to proceed for a little.'

'As your lordship pleases.'

'I think perhaps if you make an effort, madam,' repeated Maitland, who had been waiting more anxiously than he would have cared to admit for the judge's ruling, 'you will find that you remember more than you think. Was it, for instance, Mrs. Grace DeLisle who first suggested – ?'

'Oh, no, I do remember that. It wasn't Grace.'

'Mary Reynolds and Eleanor Wyatt, as the youngest members of the party, would hardly be likely to take a lead in the matter.'

'No, I suppose not.'

'Then either yourself or Mrs. Wyatt . . . perhaps she will remember, if you do not.'

'But she isn't . . . she told me she wasn't being called to give evidence.'

'There is nothing, however, to stop the defence from calling her.'

'Well, I don't think . . . anyway, I remember now. I said I was a little tired, and somehow they all decided to come up at the same time.'

'All the ladies of the party and Mr. Malcolm Harte?'

'Yes.' She gave him a smile again. 'He wouldn't be interested in the company once Mary had left it.'

'Then we come to the time – some ten minutes later, did you say? – when you saw my client descending the staircase.'

'Yes, it was twenty to eleven.'

'I must ask you, you know – my friend prepared you for the question – whether you are sure of his identity.

74

It wasn't because, so far as you knew, he was the only man of the party who had retired?'

'No. I saw him quite clearly.'

'Did he see you?'

'I think not. He was already on the staircase – '

'That raises another point,' he said quickly. 'To see him you must have gone out on the landing that connects the two wings of the house . . . may I ask, my lord, that the plan of the first floor be produced?'

There was a pause while this was done. When the judge and jury had been supplied with copies Maitland waved away the one that was offered to him. 'If you will show it to the witness, please,' he said. 'Now, madam, you will see from that quite clearly that if you had merely been going to the bathroom, as I believe you told the police in your statement, you could not possibly have seen somebody on the staircase. You would hardly have left the wing where your room was situated.'

'No, I . . . did I say that?'

'Not in this court, Lady Bowling. But certainly it was in the proof of your evidence.'

'Then . . . it doesn't really matter, does it? It seemed easier than explaining – ' She glanced round a little wildly, but Garfield, to whom she might have looked for protection, did not catch her eye. However willing he might be to interrupt, he could hardly say the matter wasn't relevant.

'Explaining what?' asked Maitland remorselessly.

'That I meant to go to the study, where I had seen some bookshelves when Grace DeLisle showed me round the house, to see if I could find something to read.'

'Not so tired after all?'

'I suppose going upstairs woke me up again. Anyway, as I said, I knew there were bookshelves in the

75

study so I thought . . . but when I saw Mr. Harte go in I decided against it and went back to my room again.'

'I see.' He was suddenly weary. So much work for so small a gain, and what did it amount to, after all? Harte had gone to the study, had been seen to go to the study, admitted that he had gone to the study. The witness's small prevarication might be peculiar, but that was as much as you could say. He found that he had seated himself, that Garfield was on his feet again, bent, no doubt, on putting the record straight. Pity he hadn't given him more to do.

Not surprisingly, perhaps, the afternoon's events had done nothing to brighten Geoffrey Horton's mood. 'While I sympathise with what you're trying to do, Antony,' he said as they were leaving the court, in a tone that, if it meant anything, meant that he was lying, 'I can't see what you hope to accomplish by antagonising the witnesses. What on earth possessed you to press the Bowling woman like that?'

'Instinct,' said Maitland. Derek Stringer, more tolerant of his leader's vagaries, even when his own advice was ignored, smiled but said nothing. But in this mood even silence did nothing to pacify Horton.

'If you can point to one single benefit –' he grumbled, but this time Maitland interrupted him without ceremony.

'We haven't even started yet,' he said, mildly enough. 'Will you do what you can this evening to arrange the interviews I mentioned to you?'

'Yes, of course. I can see we're going to have a busy weekend,' said Geoffrey, unmollified. 'Joan won't like it.'

'Neither will Jenny, but I dare say they'll both survive.'

For some reason this piece of callousness went down

well, and Horton said, quite amiably, 'I'll phone you about ten o'clock, then, and tell you what I've been able to arrange.'

'And I, in the meantime,' said Antony, 'will visit Father William.' This was a piece of pure provocation, as he knew Geoffrey didn't approve of his stated intention, but fortunately the solicitor had already said his farewells and turned away.

FRIDAY, the second day (continued)

Mr. Justice Conroy had pleased everybody, except perhaps the prisoner, by adjourning at an early hour. Maitland went back to chambers for ten minutes or so, easily avoided the temptation to confide his immediate intentions to his uncle, and decided to walk to Bedford Lane, where Mr. William Webster, known to more than his intimates as Father William, lived plainly, but to his own complete satisfaction, in rooms behind his shop.

Nothing much had changed in the five and a half years since Antony had first come there with Geoffrey. Now, as then, the window avoided anything in the nature of vulgar display, showing only a diamond pendant against dark blue velvet, and having in the background a miniature tree that somehow succeeded in looking vaguely Japanese. The girl who came forward to greet him when he pushed open the door was a stranger, however; it was a long time now since Geraldine Lindsay had left Father William's employment to become Geraldine Kellaway.

'I'm hoping to see Mr. Webster. Is he in?' But even before the girl could answer the old man himself had appeared in the doorway of the office at the back of the shop.

'Come in, Mr. Maitland, come in. Can I leave you to lock up when the time comes, Elizabeth? Then we will go into the back where we can be comfortable.'

He was a small man, white-haired, with an air of benevolent simplicity that Antony had learned long since to discount. In the living-room, which was rather sparsely furnished, he insisted on his visitor taking the one easy chair – it was, in fact, extremely comfortable – and contented himself with a hard, wooden one that he pulled out from under the table. 'It is some time since I saw you, Mr. Maitland,' he said. 'Is Mrs. Maitland well?'

'Very well, I'm glad to say.'

'And your uncle?'

'Well too.'

Father William gave him a look that said as clearly as words, Yes, I know he can be difficult at times. 'Does he know that you are here?' he asked shrewdly.

Antony laughed. 'Not that I'm here at this moment, but he knew I was coming. I told him last night when it occurred to me that perhaps you could help me.'

'I shall be only too pleased to do so, if I can.'

'Have you read about the Harte trial?'

'The jewellers' assistant whom you are defending. The papers have given it good coverage. For some reason the juxtaposition of yourself and Mr. Paul Garfield – '

'Yes, well, never mind that,' said Antony, in a hurry.

'You do not altogether relish the comparison that was made?' William Webster was not to be denied his gentle amusement, and after a moment Maitland smiled back at him.

'Not altogether,' he admitted. 'But it's about that case – '

78

'A valuation, perhaps, of the jewellery concerned.'

'That doesn't arise. The jewellery disappeared, you know.'

'Ah, but I know most of the pieces concerned. Sir Leonard Bowling would have got a bargain.'

'Would he though?' Antony was distracted momentarily from his purpose. 'Now I'd have thought the DeLisle brothers would strike a hard bargain. Even Henry, who says he is an artist.'

'And so he is, in his way,' said Father William thoughtfully. 'But some of us' – he smiled deprecatingly – 'have to be businessmen too.'

'Well, presumably they got as much as they thought they could.'

'Or as much as they thought Sir Leonard would give.'

'There wouldn't be much point in that. Another customer would have been along sooner or later.'

'Unless they had some reason for wanting it to be sooner.'

'Now, what do you mean by that?' Father William waved a hand vaguely, but said nothing. 'You've got something in mind,' Antony persisted.

'You may remember, Mr. Maitland, that I have always been averse to gossip,' said William Webster reprovingly. Antony, who remembered nothing of the kind, was almost indiscreet enough to say so; but refrained at the last moment and instead nodded sympathetically. 'But, of course, if you need my help . . . though it is difficult to see how I can help you – '

'If Harte is innocent – '

'Do you really believe he is?'

'I've come to the conclusion there's enough doubt to justify some further investigation,' said Antony lamely. For some reason, however, Father William seemed to be reassured.

'Well then, what occurred to me was this. If an insurance fraud was planned – and I think you will find, Mr. Maitland, that the jewellery was insured for considerably more than it was being sold for – it would obviously be of benefit to the claimant to be able to point to an almost-completed sale as evidence of good faith.'

'I see what you mean, of course, but it couldn't have been a conspiracy. I mean, George wouldn't have planned his own death, and if Henry was responsible it seems a little drastic . . . after all, they were brothers.'

'The best laid schemes of mice and men –' said Father William tritely. 'I'm only suggesting to you a plot that went awry.'

'Because Harte got in first? You don't think Henry might have employed him? No, that won't do,' he answered himself directly. 'Henry wouldn't be too keen on admitting to such an arrangement, but once Harte was arrested there was no reason why *he* shouldn't talk.'

'No reason but his own safety,' William Webster pointed out.

'Yes, I suppose so. I don't seem to be able to think about this case at all clearly.'

'Take your time,' said the old man kindly.

'You've certainly given me something to think about, Father William. But that wasn't . . . exactly . . . why I came to you.'

'No?' The faded blue eyes were shrewd, but still friendly. 'I wonder, Mr. Maitland, just what you think *I* can do for you.'

'I'd better explain about the prosecution's case, you can't possibly have got it clear from the papers.' It was necessary, he knew, and yet he had a guilty feeling that he was stalling. 'Harte knew as well as anybody the value of the jewellery; he was on the point of getting married, which is to say, perhaps, that he was more than usually conscious of being hard up; he had planned a continental honeymoon, ending in Amsterdam; Garfield – that's Counsel for the Prosecution – also pointed out, and Henry DeLisle confirmed, that it could not be assumed that he was without connections in that town.'

'Every man his own fence,' said Father William, smiling beatifically.

'Precisely. But that's all fairly nebulous. On the positive side we have the fact that he was seen going to the study after he had ostensibly retired, that his fingerprints were found on the open safe, of which – Henry DeLisle again – he might have known the combination.'

'That is to say that the murder wasn't premeditated, that he didn't expect to find George DeLisle standing guard over the safe.'

'I could point that out in extenuation, if he didn't deny the whole thing.' (There were no flies on Father William, he didn't need anything spelling out.) 'The final thing is that the window of the morning-room was found open, and the contention is that Harte passed the jewellery through to an accomplice before going back to bed. Certainly it was not found anywhere in the house.'

'Light is beginning to dawn, Mr. Maitland.' He sounded genuinely overjoyed. 'But perhaps it isn't too much to ask you to be a little more explicit – '

Here it came. He knows I know he's a buyer, he's never said so openly, but he's never played the hypocrite either. And I know that he knows that I know . . . but, all the same, it isn't easy. 'I thought, with your connections in the trade, you might be able to find out who the accomplice was.'

Father William was smiling his appreciation of a point delicately made. 'My connections in the trade,' he repeated, as if the phrase pleased him. 'It might be possible. And what then?'

'That's the difficult part . . . or perhaps I should say, more difficult. I want to know his principal's name.'

'That's taking a chance, isn't it? If he says it is this man Harte – '

'The position would be complicated, but that isn't your worry.'

'No, indeed. But how do you suppose I am to obtain this hypothetical accomplice's confidence?'

'I imagine you might have your own methods of doing that.'

'Well, you may be right. But confiding in me would not automatically mean that he would confide – confess to the police.' His expression was grave, but always there was the underlying current of amusement that seemed to be as much a part of his make-up as breathing. 'You should have thought of that for yourself, Mr. Maitland.'

'Strange as it may seem, I had got that far. But, don't you see, there would be two advantages? It would clear up my doubts about Harte, one way or the other. And it would mean I knew the culprit . . . a tremendous step on the way to proving it.'

'That is reasonable. But you know, Mr. Maitland, you are asking me to go to considerable pains, and while I would be only too willing if it were a personal matter, if you were in trouble yourself as you were when I first met you – '

'I haven't forgotten that I'm in your debt, rather than the other way around.'

'It is true I saved your life,' said Father William thoughtfully, 'but you in turn saved me from a charge of manslaughter – or rather, Sir Nicholas did, I am sure at your persuasion. No, I would not say that either of us owes the other anything. I have a great regard for you, Mr. Maitland – '

That, Antony thought, was true. Their friendship,

unlikely as it was, had flourished over the years. 'It is a personal matter, in a way,' he said.

'Is it?' The old man's tone was dry, but he was obviously ready to give any explanation his courteous attention. The trouble was, it wasn't easy . . .

'I have never spoken to you – I have never spoken to anybody, except once, briefly, to Uncle Nick – about my experiences during the war. Will it suffice if I tell you that they have left me with a horror, almost amounting to claustrophobia, of being shut in? Therefore, at the best of times, I have some sympathy with my clients; and when it comes to the possibility of an innocent man being imprisoned – ' He stopped there and spread his hands in a helpless gesture. 'If you don't understand, Father William, there's nothing I can say to make you,' he said.

The air of innocent gaiety had gone now, the blue eyes were troubled. 'I think I can appreciate your normal reticence,' said William Webster. 'If you feel strongly enough about this case to break your silence – '

'I do.' He had been quite right though, there was nothing more he could say. Even the effort he had made had left him drained of energy, and more conscious than usual – as always when he was tired – of the pain in his shoulder.

'Then I think I must do what I can to help you. But you do understand that I can't promise anything?'

'I understand. I can't tell you how grateful I shall be to you, though, just for trying. And I think you underestimate yourself, Father William.'

'We shall see. And now I think . . . a cup of tea, Mr. Maitland. I have an Aga cooker, you know, the kettle is always just on the boil.'

It would be ungracious to refuse, but all he wanted to do just then was to get away, somewhere alone. He wasn't a man who carried his memories lightly and consideration of the past – which he avoided whenever possible – always brought with it an incongruous sense of shame. Because there had been times when he had been deathly afraid, and he didn't want to remember . . . 'I should like that very much,' he said.

William Webster was as good as his word, and was gone only a moment. The tea was just as he liked it, hot and not too strong, with a slice of lemon; though he couldn't remember ever taking tea with Father William before, so it must be chance, not a good memory. 'It may be,' said the old man, when he had allowed his visitor to sip in silence for a while, 'that I can help you with your problem in another way.'

'How?' asked Antony hopefully.

'You have decided that Malcolm Harte is innocent – ' (Have I? thought Antony, but he did not speak his thought aloud.) ' – and therefore, as I understand it, you are looking for an alternative as the villain of the piece.'

'It is the easiest way of proving someone's innocence, certainly.' Perhaps the tea had revived him, perhaps it was just that his interest was caught, but he was suddenly less conscious of his weariness.

'Am I also right in thinking that your suspects will be drawn from the members of the party who were at the DeLisle's house in Wimbledon that night?'

'Yes, I think so. There is just a chance that some professional got wind of the fact that the jewellery would be in the house rather than in the strong-room at the shop, but I think the open window in the morning-room militates against that idea. The butler is very sure that he closed it, and Geoffrey Horton tells me there were no marks of forcible entry. Also, I think an outside job would have been pulled later in the night.'

'That sounds reasonable. The reason I ask, Mr. Maitland, is that I know something of one of the men who were staying in the house.'

'Sir Leonard Bowling?'

'No.' He ignored the sudden eagerness in Maitland's tone. 'William Wyatt,' he said. 'What do *you* know about him?'

'He's something in the city. I asked Roger about him – do you remember Roger Farrell, Father William?'

'Vividly.'

'Yes, I suppose so.' In a lighter mood the emphasis his companion put on the single word would have amused him, but now he was completely serious. 'Roger said – I think I can remember his exact words – "He would probably describe himself as a financier, which in his case would be a euphemism for money-lender".'

William Webster was, for the moment, equally serious. 'That is correct, so far as it goes,' he said. 'You will gather he is wealthy enough for his ostensible occupation to be overlooked in – er – polite circles.'

'I had gathered that, yes. You said, his *ostensible* occupation?'

'There is a rumour, a rumour I believe to be based on fact, that he is a member of that profession to which the police have been known to suspect that I belong.'

'You have to forgive them, it's their nature to be suspicious,' said Antony, who was feeling better by the minute.

'You do not ask me – '

'I'm sorry. What profession do you mean?'

Father William smiled his acknowledgement of this belated show of tact. 'That of being a buyer, Mr. Maitland, a receiver of stolen goods. There have been occasions . . . but you know and I know that it is a thing not readily susceptible of proof.'

'No, but . . . William Wyatt! He might have been after the jewellery himself.'

'I think it unlikely that he would step outside his normal role,' said Father William, in a warning tone.

85

'In that case – '

'In that case I think you must consider the possibility that your client was his tool.'

'But the open window – '

'Obviously, neither of them would want to be found with the jewellery in his possession. An associate would have received it, and later delivered it to Wyatt at his leisure.'

'Father William, was I wasting my time asking you to make enquiries? Is this something you *know*?'

'I am sure Sir Nicholas would deplore this habit of jumping to conclusions. I have said I will enquire, and I will. I am just pointing out that you shouldn't be too disappointed if the results don't come up to your expectations.'

'I see.' He was depressed again, because it did sound a reasonable theory . . . 'But Wyatt might have opened the window for an outside accomplice,' he said.

'So he might.' But there was no conviction in the old man's tone, the remark was obviously intended as a palliative. Antony drank the last of his tea and put down the cup purposefully.

'I'd better be going,' he said, with now no sign of regret in his tone. 'And again, I'm grateful . . . '

Sir Nicholas came up after dinner and Antony, letting his uncle in, took one look at his face and said, 'Friday the thirteenth, I might have known it,' in as hollow a tone as he could manage. Sir Nicholas stalked past him without deigning to notice this sally, and was already ensconced in his favourite arm-chair when Antony followed him into the living-room.

'You haven't seen fit to take my advice,' he said accusingly, as soon as his nephew appeared.

'Not . . . altogether, sir,' said Antony, repressing the desire to reply in kind.

'I've been talking to Halloran – ' ('That's obvious,' muttered Antony, to whom it was; Halloran was an old friend of Sir Nicholas's and, more than anyone else he knew, had an ear to the legal grapevine.) ' – and he tells me that this afternoon in court you were asking questions wildly, without any relevance to the case.'

'It wasn't quite as bad as that,' Antony protested. 'I admit I didn't get very far – '

'If your intention was to make a fool of yourself, I think you went quite far enough.'

'Have some coffee, Uncle Nick.' Jenny must have had a premonition, there was a third cup already on the tray. 'Have some cognac . . . oh, no, there isn't any. Give Uncle Nick some of the Cherry Brandy, Antony.'

'Abominable stuff!' Sir Nicholas was distracted, at least temporarily, from his original grievance. 'I can't think why you keep it in the house.'

'For Meg,' said Jenny patiently . . . something that Sir Nicholas knew perfectly well. She placed a cup on the table at his elbow; an ashtray and his favourite Swan Vestas were already there. Maitland was rummaging in the cupboard, and straightened with a bottle in his hand just as she added brightly, 'Antony went to see Father William after the court adjourned.' ('Taking both our lives into your hands, love,' Antony said to her afterwards, but she only smiled at him and said, 'You were going to tell him anyway.')

'Must you refer to Mr. Webster by that undignified sobriquet?'

'Everybody knows.'

'He's going to find out for me who really stole the jewellery,' said Antony casually, coming across the room with a glass in his hand. He had over-filled it, and put it down very gently. Sir Nicholas glared at it.

'I suppose I must say, Thank you,' he said disagreeably. 'As for Mr. Webster, are you sure he did not have a hand in the matter himself?'

Antony began to laugh. 'Do you know, Uncle Nick, that had never occurred to me? I think he'd have refused my request, though, if it – if it embarrassed him.'

'I never suspected you of being so naïve. There is one point, however – '

'I shall see Harte tomorrow, explain the position to him, and ask him whether he wants me to continue with my enquiries. That should take care of things . . . don't you think?'

'I suppose so.' Sir Nicholas's tone was grudging. He sipped his Cherry Brandy, and Antony half-expected another outburst, but instead he only shook his head sadly.

'Father William gave me one piece of information, anyway,' said Maitland cheerfully.

'What was that?'

'That William Wyatt is probably a fence himself.'

'In that event – '

'Yes, Father William pointed all that out to me, but it doesn't necessarily follow, you know. I rather hoped it was something about Sir Leonard Bowling that he knew – '

'I suppose by that you mean something disreputable. Why Bowling, rather than another?' For the first time, he sounded merely curious.

'Because his wife has told one little, pointless lie.'

'As you demonstrated in court this afternoon.' (Back to square one, thought Jenny resignedly, hearing all the former asperity in his voice again, and Antony ought to have known better; but Antony, who was standing with his back to, though a little to one side of, the fireplace, seemed too interested in his exposition to care about that.)

'I know you think that was a waste of time – '

'I do,' said Sir Nicholas grimly.

' – but really, Uncle Nick, I have to start some-where – '

'If we concede the necessity of starting at all.'

' – and it must have meant *something*. I mean, if she was going downstairs for a book, why not say so? No, she had something else in mind, and I wouldn't mind betting she nipped down again smartly once Harte was out of sight. Perhaps *she* opened the morning-room window. Well, at least she admitted being actually on the staircase, so we shan't have to call Eleanor Wyatt to confirm it.'

'As the point is so trivial – '

'Yes, sir, but we've been through all that once.'

Jenny said bravely into the small silence that followed this foolhardy remark, 'Do you suppose Eleanor knows that her father is a crook?'

'We don't *know* that ourselves,' said Sir Nicholas crossly. But then he had one of his sudden changes of mood and went on, quite amiably, 'I shouldn't think the child has any guilty knowledge of any kind. What is known of the rest of the party, Antony?'

'I haven't been able to get any real light on George DeLisle's character – '

'As the motive seems to have been theft, that prob-ably doesn't matter.'

'All the same, I should like . . . Henry DeLisle de-scribes himself as an artist in his trade, but I think he has an eye to the main chance too. Father William sug-gested the possibility of an insurance fraud, but I don't see how that could have gone wrong enough to leave George dead. Grace DeLisle seems like a simple house-wife, not too intelligent, very conscious of her husband's wishes in making her arrangements, but with a kind heart that sometimes gets the better of her. Mary Reynolds is a little prude – '

'And none the worse for that, I dare say,' remarked his uncle.

'Well, I don't know. She knew perfectly well why Harte wanted to be at the DeLisles' with her, and if it wasn't leading him on to accept the invitation I don't know what you'd call it. And then I doubt if she gave him so much as a goodnight kiss!'

'This so-called permissive society – '

'Yes, Uncle Nick. Neither Jenny nor I is in need of one of your lectures on that subject.' Jenny got up quietly to refill Sir Nicholas's glass; she was smiling as she did so, but either he did not see the smile or he chose to ignore it.

'I can see that I have something, at least, to be thankful for.' His tone was gently sarcastic, but compared with his mood when he arrived he was now – as Antony put it mentally – a thing of sweetness and light. 'You were telling me about Mary Reynolds, Antony. If you can do so without maligning the girl – '

'She was scrupulous about telling the truth under oath – '

'Which must count as a virtue.'

'I agree. But she needn't have been quite so keen to tell the police everything in the first place, and if she hadn't spelled it all out for them Garfield would have had no basis for the questions he asked. She's clearly made up her mind that Harte is guilty – '

'In which she may show her wisdom.'

'Well, if she was in love with the chap she ought at least to show some confidence in him,' Antony maintained stubbornly. 'Whatever anybody else may think, whatever the truth is.'

'You have taken a dislike to the girl, probably an unreasonable dislike.'

'I'm afraid that's true.'

'But at least you won't suggest that she had anything

to do with the crime, either as principal or accessary.'

'No. For one thing, she'd have been round at the police station confessing her sins before the blood was dry; for another, from the medical evidence this wasn't a woman's murder. The amount of force used – '

'May I remind you that these details are not pleasant for Jenny?'

'I'm sorry.' But Jenny, when he looked at her, had still her serene look. She was tougher than Uncle Nick chose to think. 'Anyway, you can take my word for it.'

'With pleasure. Now, if I remember correctly what Halloran told me, the last witness today was Lady Bowling.'

'The divine Sarah!' Antony risked a recurrence of his learned relative's ire by grinning as he spoke. 'She called herself a housewife, too, but that was by way of a joke, I gather. I can't see her dishing up the potatoes, or making the bed, or even going round with a duster.'

'Is she very beautiful?' asked Jenny. 'That's what the papers say.'

'And they're right, I don't think there's any other word for it. I can understand her husband's desire to deck her out in gems, in a way.'

'Which he is fortunate to be able to indulge,' said Sir Nicholas austerely. But there seemed to be no malice in the remark; he smiled from one to the other of them in quite a friendly way.

'Well, that's just the point. Is he?'

'Is he what?'

'Able to indulge himself in that way. Fifty thousand pounds is a lot of money, and now I come to think of it I suppose it would have been more than that by the time the new designs were made up.'

'As much as that? But surely . . . what is known of him, Antony?'

'He's a newspaper tycoon. Is that the right phrase?'

'To convey your meaning, it will do as well as another. He owns that regrettable rag the *Evening Chronicle*; also the *Courier*, which you are so misguided as to insist on reading.'

'For old times' sake, Dad worked for them,' Antony protested.

'I had not forgotten. It was under different management then, and has certainly not improved.'

'I'll grant you that. I don't think they actually lose money but the thing is, with today's difficulties, do they earn enough to make Bowling a very wealthy man?'

'They may have made sufficient in the past to ensure his wealth today.'

'That's all very well, but it is a thought, Uncle Nick.'

'Guesswork,' said Sir Nicholas succinctly. Antony knew his opinion of that, without being told, and went on to the next point without delay.

'I've told you about Wyatt. Or did I ever tell you Roger says his brand of finance is money-lending?'

'Not that I remember.'

'Well, it is. His wife, whom I seem to remember is called Rose, is an unknown quantity, but as we've decided it's a man's crime perhaps that doesn't matter.' Sir Nicholas let that pass. 'That leaves us with the two men who weren't staying in the house. I wonder if either of them had the opportunity of opening the morning-room window before they left. It would be a help if I could talk to Sykes.'

'Chief Inspector Sykes was the investigating officer, wasn't he? I hope you will not attempt anything so improper.'

'Give me credit for some sense, Uncle Nick. Not much, but some.' His uncle surprised him by smiling at him, unexpectedly and companionably. 'Godfrey Thurlow is Eleanor Wyatt's employer, and I don't know anything about him except that the Sefton Gallery has a good reputation, and somebody said he preferred the old settings for the jewels to the new designs Henry DeLisle had made.'

'You'll be telling me next that he might have committed the crime to preserve the status quo,' said Sir Nicholas sardonically.

'That hadn't occurred to me, but I'll bear it in mind.'

'Don't you dare to take me seriously!'

'Weren't you serious?' asked Antony, with intent to annoy. 'Finally we have Laurence Blake, who may or may not be engaged to Eleanor – '

'You didn't tell me that, Antony,' Jenny put in.

'Didn't I? He said he wouldn't want anything more to do with her if she came to me on Malcolm Harte's behalf. In any case, she seems to have got herself into a bit of a muddle; because I should say myself – wouldn't you, Uncle Nick? – that she's more than half in love with my client.'

'Well, Mary Reynolds has thrown him over, so perhaps – '

'He's being tried for murder, love. First things first.'

'Yes, I know, but – ' Jenny began, to be ruthlessly interrupted by Sir Nicholas.

'I think Antony is right, my dear, you should postpone your match-making until the position has clarified a little.'

'I was only – ' said Jenny, but broke off when Sir Nicholas smiled at her. 'Oh, well!' she said.

'What is known of Laurence Blake, Antony, besides his apparent lack of chivalry?'

'He's a crime reporter for the *Courier*.'

'Then you should know something of him.'

'He writes well . . . factually, not too much speculation. Unless he has private means he's a bit out of his class with the Wyatts and the Bowlings, but unless it's

93

a matter of keeping up with the Joneses his marriage to Eleanor should put him on easy street financially. I don't imagine she'll come to him penniless.'

'And that is all – '

'I hope to know more about all of them – the people the prosecution hasn't called – before the weekend's out.'

'I wish you joy of the task.' Sir Nicholas picked up his empty glass and eyed it pensively for a moment. 'I wonder, Jenny,' he said then, 'whether Meg's visits have left you with any more of this singularly repellent liquid.'

SATURDAY, the weekend recess

As promised, Geoffrey had phoned the previous evening, and the visit to the prison was fixed for ten o'clock. As Malcolm Harte joined them in the interview room Maitland eyed him with renewed interest. The prisoner was, as he had noted before, at the same time good-looking and insignificant; yet if he had done what the prosecution alleged . . . you couldn't tell, of course, those quiet, small men could be driven to desperation as easily as anyone else. That was what he had thought the first time he had seen him, with Geoffrey only too eager to convince him of his client's innocence. Perhaps that had been the trouble, though he wouldn't like to think of himself as quite so wrong-headed. Now he was taking a second look, seeing Harte through Eleanor Wyatt's eyes perhaps, noting the signs of strain (well, that might mean anything!), the brown eyes wary, the lips clamped tightly together as though there was something that their owner did not want to reveal.

If the man was innocent . . . but wasn't he doing for

94

himself now what he had suspected Geoffrey of trying to do before, convincing himself on no real evidence . . .

And here was Harte, unexpectedly taking the initiative while counsel was still wondering how to begin. He had made no reply to Horton's greeting except to nod abruptly, and now said, his eyes on Maitland's face, 'I didn't think you'd want to see me again.'

'In the circumstances, it seemed advisable – '

'What circumstances?'

Horton glanced rather helplessly at his friend, but if Maitland was at all put out by this rather unconventional greeting he wasn't showing it. Instead he laughed, which was a thing Geoffrey never remembered him doing in a prison interview room before, and said lightly, 'Do you want to quarrel with me, Mr. Harte?'

That brought, for several seconds, no response. Then Harte said, no less antagonistically, 'I suppose you think I should be grateful to you for taking the time to see me.'

Geoffrey Horton started to say something, but caught a look from Maitland and thought better of it. 'I think we'd better call a truce for the moment,' said Antony, still amused. 'Won't you both sit down?'

He thought for a moment that Malcolm was going to refuse this simple request, but after regarding his counsel in silence for a while he pulled out the chair at the end of the table nearest the door and seated himself. Geoffrey followed suit, but Maitland remained standing, his hands resting lightly on the back of the chair in front of him. 'I can enlighten you very simply as to the circumstances,' he said. 'But I should like to know first what I've done to offend you.'

'You didn't believe me when I told you I was innocent, did you?'

'I . . . reserved judgment.'

'And now you're beginning to wonder . . . I didn't

95

expect the sort of questions you asked in court yesterday.'

'If that is what has upset you – ' Antony's tone was
still light, but he looked, to Horton's eye, to be a little
taken aback.

'Well, it is. Can't you understand what it's like to
have people sitting in judgment on you? Even you,
whom I hoped to convince – '

'When you put it like that,' said Maitland soberly, 'I
can understand it very well indeed. But I'm afraid what
I have to say to you will offend you still further.'

That brought a gleam of what looked like humour to
Malcolm's eye. 'You'd better try me,' he said.

'For reasons I'll go into in a moment I've decided to
put in hand further enquiries over and above what is
called for by my brief. I want to know whether I have
your agreement for this course of action.'

'You're thinking these enquiries of yours may uncover something incriminating to me.'

It was no use mincing words. 'Precisely,' said Maitland, and waited to see what the reaction would be.

Strangely, Harte's tone seemed to reflect a simple
curiosity. 'Supposing you decide when you've finished
that you're even more convinced of my guilt . . . what
then?'

'We should proceed as planned at present. Barring a
confession from you it would still be only my opinion,
I shouldn't *know*.'

'These fine distinctions!'

Antony smiled at him. 'That's very much what my
wife always says when the subject comes up,' he said.
'But you shouldn't be worrying about what *I* think, you
know. In the long run it's what the jury decide that
matters.'

'Well, I do worry. I suppose you're thinking now, if
he's innocent what's all the fuss about?'

96

'Something like that,' Maitland admitted.

'The thing is, accidentally I suppose – it must be accidentally – appearances are so much against me that I can't help wondering if whatever else you uncover may be equally misleading.'

'I see. Are you trying to tell me now you think you've been framed?'

'No. I'm just trying to explain – '

'The victim of circumstances, then?' said Antony, and smiled again, but not as though he were amused.

'I think you understand very well what I mean,' said Malcolm without heat.

'Perhaps I do. Do I call off the enquiries I've already instigated?'

'No!'

'Very well. We shall proceed on the course Mr. Horton has mapped out for us. But first – '

'You haven't told me why your attitude changed.'

'Yes, I suppose you would be curious about that. I had a visitor on Thursday evening . . . Eleanor Wyatt.'

'Eleanor? I don't quite understand.'

'She told me, "He wouldn't do a thing like that",' said Antony. He tried to keep his voice expressionless but could hear, in spite of this, a sardonic note in it. Harte heard it too, and for the first time a tinge of colour came into his cheeks. 'You needn't laugh at her,' he said.

'I'm not, believe me. It's only that I've had the same thing said to me a hundred times, or more.'

'In that case, I can't see why you took any notice. I shouldn't take you for a credulous man.'

'I don't think I am. It's difficult to explain, but she made me see that perhaps I hadn't been quite fair to you in deciding there was nothing to be done about the case except speak to my brief. You see, you were quite right when you accused me of sitting in judgment. I might apologise for that, but it's asking rather a lot of human nature – '

Malcolm seemed to have forgotten his grievance. He said, frowning, 'I don't see what else you *can* do.'

No need to bring Father William into it. 'For one thing, I can talk to the other people who were present that evening . . . the ones who aren't being called to give evidence.'

'I don't see what good that will do.'

'Neither do I, yet. But Miss Wyatt told me one thing, you know . . . that Lady Bowling had actually been on her way downstairs when you went into the study.'

'I thought you were just guessing, and I don't see what good it did anyway.'

'That is something we can't know until all the evidence is in.'

'No, of course. I didn't mean to sound ungracious. But tell me about Eleanor. Did Laurence come with her?'

'No, she was courageous enough to come alone.'

'I don't suppose he liked her mixing herself up in something like this.'

'I gathered there had been some disagreement between them.'

'I'm sorry about that. You won't . . . I don't want her to get mixed up in all this.'

'No need. Lady Bowling has already admitted the only thing Miss Wyatt could tell us.'

'That's good. Not that I can blame Laurence for thinking what everyone else thinks. You could tell by the witnesses so far. Even Mary – '

'If we can prove your innocence – ' said Maitland briskly, because he was suddenly almost intolerably sorry for the prisoner, and sympathy wasn't an emotion he could afford.

'I don't see how you can do that. Even if you get me

off, which doesn't seem likely, I shouldn't have a job, nothing to offer her. And to tell you the truth I don't think I could ever feel the same again. She, at least, could have believed me.'

Unfair to raise hope where there was so little. 'Let's cross our bridges as we come to them,' Antony suggested. 'Meanwhile, Mr. Harte, there is the little matter of your own evidence.'

'Will they . . . will it be soon?'

'The prosecution have only one more witness, so far as I know: Chief Inspector Sykes.'

'I liked him, you know. I even thought he believed what I told him. But obviously he didn't.'

'After that,' said Maitland, ignoring this by-path, 'I shall open briefly for the defence, and then it will be your turn.'

'On Monday, then?'

'Most likely. Now, you've made a very clear statement, there's nothing for you to worry about, if we can just get one point straightened out.'

'What is that?' He sounded wary now, and the colour was back in his face again.

'Why you went down to the study to see George DeLisle.'

'I told you – '

'You told me there was a point about the date of your holiday you wanted to get cleared up. Quite frankly, Mr. Harte, I don't believe you, and I don't think the jury will either.'

'I don't see what's so difficult about it.'

'Don't you?' (Geoffrey, watching them, saw the elusive likeness to Sir Nicholas for the moment very strong.) 'Then perhaps I'd better explain. You heard Miss Reynolds's evidence, your honeymoon trip had been carefully planned, the dates fixed for some time. What could there be still to check?'

'He – George DeLisle – he'd said on Friday that perhaps we couldn't go when we'd arranged.'

'Did you tell Miss Reynolds that?'

'No.'

'Or anybody else?'

'No.'

'And why, if you wished to take the matter up with him again – '

'I wanted to try and persuade him to change his mind.'

'Why then? Why not at the office on Monday morning?'

'I wanted to see him alone.'

'Yes that, at least, I suppose to be the truth. Very well, Mr. Harte, if you won't tell me, you won't tell me. But you'd better be very clear on that point in your own mind before Garfield gets up to cross-examine you.'

'If I can't make you believe me – '

'Perhaps my learned friend for the prosecution will be more – what was your word? – credulous, wasn't it?'

'I can't do anything but tell the truth.'

'You'll be on oath on Monday,' Maitland reminded him.

'Yes.' He'd known it before, of course, but now the realisation struck him anew and it shook him, that was obvious.

'Miss Wyatt says you're a churchgoer.'

'Yes, I'm a Catholic.'

'Then swearing should mean more to you than a mere form of words. Think it over.' He felt more sympathetic than he sounded, the advice came abruptly. 'And now, Mr. Harte, as long as we're here we'll just go over your evidence one more time. From the beginning . . . '

'Do you suppose,' said Geoffrey, as they left the prison together and strolled towards the place where he had left the car, 'that the poor chap feels any the better for our visit?'

'That wasn't the object of the exercise. However – '

'I know it's unreasonable of him to seem to resent what you're trying to do.'

'I was telling the truth when I told him I could understand that. I'd be glad enough to cheer him up, Geoffrey, I'm not quite heartless,' – Horton had a smile for that, but he hid it from his companion – 'but it wouldn't be a kindness to offer him too much hope.'

'You needn't have bullied him, however.'

'If you mean about the reason for his visit to the study – '

'I can't see why you don't believe him.'

'Do you?'

'Y-yes.'

'Come now, of the two of us you're usually the sceptical one.'

'Why don't you believe him?'

'For the reasons I gave, and because of his obvious uneasiness over that part of his evidence. What's more, Garfield will see it as I do, and if you think I bullied Harte, Geoffrey, wait till you hear what *he*'ll have to say.'

'I suppose you're right.' Horton sighed and glanced at his watch. 'We proceed as planned, then. Wyatt and Bowling this afternoon.' They reached the car as he spoke, and he paused with his hand on the door handle. 'We've just time for lunch.'

'Jenny's expecting us. Uncle Nick will probably be there too, as it's really our day for going to him.'

'What does he have to say about all this?'

'He is not amused.' Antony got into the car. 'Don't bring the subject up, that's all. He may have said all he has to say about it last night, though I shouldn't count on that, if I were you.'

The Wyatts had what you could only recognise as a good address in Belgravia, in a house that had been divided much more subtly than the one in Kempenfeldt Square, to give each family occupying it its own front door. William Wyatt was expecting them, and he and his wife, Rose, were awaiting them in the big drawing-room, a comfortable, chintzy place in which it would be only too easy, Antony felt, to sink into one of the arm-chairs and never emerge from its embrace again.

Wyatt was a compact man of middle height, care-fully dressed without the faintest hint of the casual. Maitland recognised the tie of a famous public school, and wondered ... the accent when he greeted them was unobtrusive, he couldn't place it, but certainly it wasn't what one would expect. Mrs. Wyatt, a pretty woman with fair, rather curly hair, was also neatly attired, in a dark blue dress that he mentally labelled 'dress for interviewing lawyers in'. He had the thought that they were both concerned with the impression they made. The whole set-up smelt of money; it would be interest-ing to know where it came from, and how far Father William had been right. He realised without surprise that, if it came to a pinch, he would be quite willing to rely on the old man's word.

Greetings were exchanged. 'I know you by reputa-tion,' said Wyatt, which gave Geoffrey a moment's un-easiness, knowing how his friend generally reacted to remarks like that. But Antony was speaking to Mrs. Wyatt, and only a quick frown betrayed his feelings. Then they were all seated – and no one had dis-appeared completely! – and Wyatt was going on smoothly, 'I admit I was a little surprised at this request for a meeting. I should have thought, if it was necessary at all, that you would have wanted to see us a good deal sooner.'

'Something came up,' said Maitland vaguely, before Horton, who had his own explanation prepared, could speak. It looked as if Eleanor hadn't told her parents of her visit to Kempenfeldt Square, and if that was the case he didn't want to give her away. 'I felt as if I weren't getting a clear enough picture in court of the events of that evening. It might be useful to get your impressions.'

'I don't see what we can tell you that Grace and Henry DeLisle couldn't,' said Rose Wyatt, looking puzzled.

'Let's try, at any rate. You arrived at the Wimbledon house – '

'I'm not sure of the time, are you, William?' Wyatt shook his head. 'But we aimed to be there at half past six, so I suppose it would be somewhere about that time.'

'What happened then?'

'It was a very quiet evening, really.' Rose looked at her husband helplessly, and he took up the tale.

'We were shown into the drawing-room for a few minutes, before Grace took us up to our room. We only stayed there long enough for Rose to tidy her hair, and then went downstairs again. Leonard and Sarah – the Bowlings – were there with the three DeLisles. Also young Harte and the secretary-girl, Mary Reynolds. I didn't think Henry was best pleased about that, and certainly they seemed a little out of their depth.'

'But they're both very quiet, well-behaved young people,' Rose put in. 'At least, that's what we thought until this dreadful thing happened.'

'Malcolm is these gentlemen's client,' said William, smiling. 'You mustn't imply that he's guilty . . . or not yet.'

'Well, I'm sorry, but – ' She broke off and looked from one of them to the other. 'I know you have to do your best for him, but I didn't think there was any doubt about it,' she said.

'He has pleaded Not Guilty,' Maitland pointed out, 'so perhaps for the time being – '

'I wish he were innocent, I can tell you,' said Rose Wyatt with feeling. 'Grace has been blaming herself so much for inviting him to stay.'

'Did you know that Mary Reynolds has broken off her engagement?' Antony asked.

'Yes, Eleanor told us.'

'You may say, circumstances did that for her,' said Wyatt dryly.

'I didn't blame her, anyway,' said Mrs. Wyatt. 'I don't see what else she could do. But if he didn't do it after all – '

'You're jumping to conclusions again, my dear. Neither Mr. Maitland nor Mr. Horton has said anything to make us think – ' He stopped there, and gave Antony a quizzical look; and Antony said, putting forward the suggestion with the diffident air that could be so misleading,

'Perhaps we could all keep an open mind until the verdict is in.'

'Certainly, certainly.' Wyatt's agreement was perhaps over-cordial. 'You were asking about that evening – '

'You had arrived, and found some of the guests gathered together.'

'That's right. Thurlow and my future son-in-law, Laurence Blake, arrived within a few minutes of each other. Again, I can't tell you exactly when, but they had time for a drink before dinner. There was really nothing special about the evening at all, nothing that stands out.'

'It's times I'm concerned with, more than anything else. Though, of course,' Maitland added, smiling, 'if there were any sinister undertones – '

'That's just what I mean. Nothing!'

'Then just fill in the time-table for me.'

'It was ten o'clock – we'd had dinner, and the coffee things had been cleared away – when George DeLisle fetched the jewellery. I didn't know at the time that there was a safe in the study, though I suppose I might have assumed it. Anyway, we spent an interesting half-hour examining the jewellery, and the sketches which Henry put forward as suggestions for re-setting the various pieces.'

'Were you all interested in what was on show?'

'The ladies more than the men, I believe. Though, of course, Leonard, as the prospective purchaser – '

'Mr. Thurlow was interested too,' his wife interrupted him. 'But he said as far as he was concerned it was vandalism to break up the present settings.'

'What had Mr. Henry DeLisle to say to that?'

Rose Wyatt laughed. Her laugh, like her voice, was pleasant. 'He was . . . just a little huffy, I believe. But, of course, Mr. Thurlow was a guest, so he couldn't really say anything.'

'And when you had all looked your fill – ?'

'George took the jewellery away again.' William Wyatt took up the thread of the narrative. 'He didn't mean to return, not for some time anyway. Said he had letters to write.'

'Didn't that strike you as rather odd?'

'Not as we were staying in the house, and Grace and Henry were there to entertain us. You're thinking perhaps he might have made an arrangement to see . . . somebody . . . in the study.'

'Something of the sort had crossed my mind.' (And if Wyatt adds thought-reading to his other accomplishments, he's a very formidable character indeed.)

'We know that Malcolm went in to see him.'

'So we do,' agreed Maitland noncommittally.

Wyatt went on without any further prompting. 'George's retirement seemed to break the party up. Within a few minutes Mr. Thurlow and Laurence left together, and immediately after that the ladies went up to bed. Oh, and I should say that Malcolm left us at the same time.'

'Did that surprise you?'

'No, he wouldn't be interested in our conversation, and once the other young people had gone – '

'That brings me to another point, Mr. Wyatt. Forget what happened for a moment; what did you think of Malcolm Harte before that tragic weekend?'

'I hardly knew him.'

'He was a friend of your daughter's, however.'

'Mary and Eleanor have known each other for a long time. But as for Malcolm – ' He shrugged.

'He seemed a well-behaved young man,' said Rose, not very helpfully.

'You had no objection to the acquaintance?'

'No objection in the world.' But her husband qualified that by saying shortly,

'If Eleanor chose to waste her own and Laurence's time with a penniless and not very interesting young couple, there was nothing I could do about it.'

'I see. I wonder if that means that you had remonstrated with her on occasion.'

'She said she liked them both.'

'And Mr. Blake?'

'Laurence? He would do what Eleanor wanted, I suppose.'

'Then may we go back to the evening of June thirteenth?'

'I've practically finished. We – '

'Perhaps I could hear from Mrs. Wyatt first. It was Lady Bowling who first suggested retiring, I believe.'

'Was it? I don't seem to remember that. I thought it would be a good idea to leave the men alone together, then if Leonard and Henry had any further business they wanted to discuss they could do so without interruption.'

'So you all went upstairs together?'

'Yes.'

'And you went to your own room; did you see or hear anything unusual after that?'

'Nothing. Eleanor had my sleeping pills, and she brought them to me, but you can't be interested in that.'

'Then we will return to the drawing-room again. Mr. Wyatt?'

'There's nothing to tell you. We had a nightcap, and some conversation – nothing more about the jewellery, I didn't expect it.'

'Why not?'

'Because both Leonard and Henry are far too wise to show over-much interest in a deal that is in the making.'

'I'm sorry I interrupted you. Go on.'

'There's nowhere to go. We went up to bed at eleven-thirty, I can tell you that because Leonard remarked on the time. And then there was nothing till the disturbance when Henry went down to the study.'

'But before that, during the period that you and Sir Leonard Bowling and Mr. Henry DeLisle were in the drawing-room together, did none of you leave the room?'

'That isn't the sort of thing one remembers after all this time.'

'Mr. DeLisle said in court that though he himself had not left the room both of his companions had done so at one time or another.'

'I suppose he has had more occasion than either of us to think over the events of that evening.' That came smoothly enough, but Maitland thought the questions now were causing Wyatt some uneasiness.

'You think then that Sir Leonard would not remember either?'

'How can I possibly tell?' He sounded indignant.

'I'm sorry to press the point, but now you come to think about it – '

Wyatt sighed impatiently. 'I really cannot see the point of these questions.'

'Oh, my dear, Mr. Maitland wants to establish that someone besides Malcolm had the opportunity to murder George.' (Now, that was funny. He hadn't imagined that Rose Wyatt had a scrap of malice in her.)

'Is that true?' Wyatt demanded. There was nothing vague about his indignation now.

'Mrs. Wyatt is reading too much into what are, after all, very basic questions. I gather that from the drawing-room nothing could be heard of what went on in the study, but someone crossing the hall – '

'That seems reasonable.' Wyatt might have been mollified, but the uneasiness remained. 'I can tell you that when I went out I heard nothing – '

'On your way to and from the downstairs cloak-room?'

'Exactly.'

'And saw nothing either.'

'No.'

'Well, you have remembered so much at least. Can you also remember the time?'

'Except that it must have been early in the proceedings, not long after the ladies went up to bed.'

'While Harte was in the study, perhaps?'

'Very likely.'

'And Sir Leonard's absence?'

'Now I think about it I do remember. Henry had just asked me to have another drink, and I glanced at my watch before I agreed. That was just after Leonard came back.'

'What time, then?'

'About three minutes to eleven.'

'Thank you. There is only one other thing . . . you remember Sir Leonard coming back into the drawing-room. How long had he been absent?'

'I think,' said Wyatt with a flash of venom, 'that you are not being completely honest with me, Mr. Maitland. My wife's assessment of your intentions was probably correct.'

That was something he would neither confirm nor deny. 'It can do no harm, however, to answer my question,' Antony pointed out.

'Very well.' That sounded ominous. 'As far as I recall he was absent – as I was myself – for no more than two or three minutes.'

Maitland got to his feet, a little regretfully. It was obvious that any further queries wouldn't be met with much tolerance, but perhaps, after all, he'd got as much as he had a right to expect. Wyatt was lying about something, the only question was, What? And how he could use it he didn't see.

Rose Wyatt smiled at him seraphically as he made his farewells, and he tried to return the smile without rancour. If she felt that her husband needed some protection . . .

Wyatt only acknowledged their goodbyes by nodding unsmilingly, but he saw them himself to the door, and shut it behind them rather more firmly than might have been considered polite.

'You handled that very nicely,' said Horton cordially, as they made their way back to the car again. 'You did no more than make an enemy – or perhaps two – for life.'

Antony laughed. It was a relief to be back in the fresh air again, and a pale sun was struggling through the mist. 'That doesn't worry me over much,' he said, 'though I could have done without Mrs. Wyatt's intervention. But you mustn't be sarcastic about my poor efforts, Geoffrey. It doesn't become you.'

Sir Leonard Bowling was younger than Antony had expected, probably in his early forties, but otherwise he fitted well enough into his mental picture of what a newspaper proprietor should be. Bowling was fair, and of middle height; carelessly elegant, as though he observed Beau Brummel's rule of being perfect when he left his dressing-room, and never giving his appearance a moment's thought after that. He and his wife lived in an expensively converted mews cottage, not far from the Wyatts' home, but Lady Bowling was not present when they were shown into a small room on the ground floor that gave the impression of being peculiarly a masculine domain. Which saved some tedious explanations.

And, as Wyatt had done, Sir Leonard said the worst possible thing in response to Geoffrey's introduction of himself and his companion. 'I've heard of you, Mr. Maitland.' He sounded as if it was a matter for congratulation, but Antony said only,

'Have you, though?' unhelpfully. And then, 'I feel, and Mr. Horton agrees with me, that it would be helpful to get your impressions of the evening of the murder.'

'I don't see what good it will do you. If the newspapers are anything to go on, all that must have been gone into exhaustively in court.'

'You are not basing that opinion solely on a perusal of the papers, I imagine.'

'No, I have been interested enough to talk to the reporters concerned.'

'And Lady Bowling no doubt informed you – '
Antony's manner was at its most diffident, but to
Geoffrey's mind he seemed intent on stirring up trouble.
Now he paused, and Sir Leonard spoke rather quickly
to fill the silence.

'I have not discussed the matter with my wife.'

'I see.' He smiled then, and left the subject; to
Geoffrey's relief (perhaps there was something in tele-
pathy, after all!). 'I forget the name of the reporter who
is covering the trial for the *Courier*, but it isn't Laurence
Blake.'

'Naturally not.'

'He isn't being called by either the defence or the
prosecution. I should have thought – '

'In the circumstances, it would have been most un-
suitable.'

'He's a good man, though, isn't he?'

'An excellent reporter.' There was no doubt
about it, for some reason he disliked the subject. His
voice was stiff. Maitland went on as though he hadn't
noticed.

'You see, we shall be seeing him tomorrow, and I
thought as his employer you could probably tell me
what sort of chap he is.' He's up to something, Geoffrey
thought gloomily; he had rarely heard his friend sound
so disingenuous.

'I can tell you nothing about him. He does his work,
that is all that concerns me.'

'You met him at the DeLisles' house that night in
June. Was that the first time you had encountered him
socially?'

'No, it was not. All the same . . . really, Mr. Maitland,
I thought it was matters of fact you were concerned
with, not my opinion.'

'So I am, but bear with me for a moment.' He hesitated, as though uncertain how to proceed. 'You met a

man called Godfrey Thurlow at the DeLisles' that evening. Was he previously known to you?'

'I had never met him before.'

'Do you know if Lady Bowling – ?'

'She may have visited the Sefton Gallery. I really couldn't say.'

'Tell me then . . . I asked Lady Bowling in court whether you were in negotiation for an alternative set of jewels to the ones that were lost to you. She didn't seem to know.'

'She didn't know because there is nothing to know.' He was angry, and for some reason trying hard to hide it. 'The whole thing was a bit of a shock, you know. In a way I felt responsible.'

'Why?'

'Because if I hadn't arranged to see the jewellery at his home, George DeLisle would still be alive.'

'It is his murder, then, not the loss of the jewels, that concerns you?'

'Of course!'

'Even though you had made a commitment to Lady Bowling?'

'Mr. Maitland!' For a moment his anger flared, unconcealed. (But he doesn't throw us out, thought Geoffrey, and that's odd.) 'That is a matter, surely, between myself and my wife,' Sir Leonard went on, more quietly.

'Let us turn then,' said Antony, ignoring the anger as he had ignored the earlier stiffness, 'to those matters of fact that you think are so important.'

'I don't.'

'No, you merely think I should concern myself with them exclusively. What happened on the night of the thirteenth of June, after the ladies and Malcolm Harte retired?'

'Nothing at all. We had a drink, the three of us who

remained, and some conversation, and went to bed ourselves about an hour later.'

'What did you talk about?'

'For heaven's sake! If you expect me to remember at this distance of time – '

'I had thought that perhaps the events of that evening would have proved particularly memorable.'

'Not in the case of some quite desultory conversation.'

'Never mind. Let us try instead a more important point. Both your companions are agreed that during the hour in question you and Wyatt both left the drawing-room at one time or another.'

'That is quite likely. Yes, I think that is correct. But I don't see – '

'Nothing that went on in the study could be heard from the drawing-room, I understand, but someone crossing the hall – '

'That seems reasonable,' said Bowling, relaxing a little. 'But unless Wyatt heard anything I'm afraid it isn't very helpful. My own excursion was quite uneventful.'

'You returned to the drawing-room, Mr. Wyatt tells me, at three minutes to eleven.'

'Did I? I'm afraid I couldn't be so exact about it.'

'So, you see, if you had heard anything from the study it would have been after my client left it.'

'I tell you, I was nowhere near the study door.'

'And Mr. Wyatt . . . when did he absent himself?'

Sir Leonard made a show of thinking that over. 'Not long before we went upstairs. Just a few minutes before, if I remember.'

'Thank you. You say you were nowhere near the study door, Sir Leonard. Did you by any chance pass the morning-room?'

'Certainly not!' That was said heatedly, but he continued more calmly after a moment. 'I am not even sure where the morning-room is situated.'

'Immediately behind the drawing-room, on the same side of the hall.'

'In that case – ' He shrugged, and left the sentence there. 'I'm afraid you're not getting much satisfaction from my answers, Mr. Maitland.'

'You might be surprised,' said Antony vaguely. 'There's just one more thing, and then I won't trouble you any further.' He came to his feet as he spoke. 'Why do you think your wife lied to the court about her reason for leaving her room? And don't tell me it was from feelings of delicacy, because I wouldn't believe you.'

'She told you herself – '

'You said you hadn't spoken together on the subject,' said Maitland quickly.

'I also mentioned that I had talked with the reporter who is covering the case.'

'Anyway, as far as her explanation is concerned, she only gave it after I had demonstrated quite clearly that her first statement must be untrue.'

Sir Leonard was on his feet as well. 'I am glad you said that was your last question,' he said coldly, 'because I shouldn't like to disoblige you. But I really think I've given you enough of my time.'

Geoffrey was silent as they drove back to Kempen-feldt Square, but as they got out of the car he said what was in his mind. 'When you're in this mood, Antony, you terrify me.'

'Come now,' said Maitland encouragingly. 'A few hard words, a little coolness in the atmosphere. No harm done.'

'Do you really think Bowling conspired with his wife to steal the jewellery? Because all I can say is that the evidence is very slim.'

Annoyingly, Antony was vague again. 'One had to begin somewhere,' he said, and produced his latch-key and opened the door with a flourish. For a wonder, Gibbs was nowhere to be seen. 'You'll feel better for some tea,' Maitland added, as Geoffrey followed him up the steps. But it took a good deal of cajolery on Jenny's part to bring the solicitor back to his customary good humour.

SUNDAY, the weekend recess

On Sunday morning the sun still shone, faint but persistent, and Jenny and Antony took a walk in the park after breakfast. Antony was thoughtful, though, and inclined not to answer Jenny's remarks until, in some cases, several minutes had elapsed. She took this patiently, only reserving the right to repeat such information as she had given him at a later date; and hoping that he would keep out of Sir Nicholas's way until such time as the trial was over, or he had come to some conclusion that would do away with the necessity for further rumination.

They had an early lunch, and had barely finished when Geoffrey Horton arrived. The appointment with Laurence Blake was for two o'clock, and they had to get out to Streatham where he had a service flat in a newish block of apartments. Maitland was surprised when they arrived there, prompt almost to the second, to find a degree of elegance in the reporter's accommodation that he would not have thought affordable on a newspaper salary. Perhaps it was a better-paying job than he had imagined; perhaps Blake had private means. It didn't really matter. First there was the awkward question of conciliating the witness.

Blake received them unsmilingly. 'You're here because of this nonsense of Eleanor's, aren't you?' he said. He was a tall man, the description 'well-built' might be as good as any other; also 'handsome', and with the personality to impress that fact on anyone who came into contact with him. He had dark, wavy hair, collar-length at the back, and with fashionable sideburns; altogether, thought Antony a little sourly, the answer to a maiden's prayer.

'It was Miss Wyatt who made me see the necessity of looking twice at the facts,' he answered mildly. Laurence did not seem much impressed by this effort at diplomacy.

'I should have thought myself the facts were obvious,' he said.

'If you feel like that, I'm surprised you were willing to see us.'

'I've learned something of your reputation through my work, Mr. Maitland. Let's say I was curious.'

Heard something of me, and written about me yourself on occasion. Perhaps it was this unfortunate remark that prompted Antony to forget the careful approach he had intended. 'Are you still engaged to Eleanor Wyatt?' he enquired abruptly.

'Now, how in the world can that concern you?'

'Let's say I'm curious too.' There was very little mirth about the smile he gave Laurence Blake at this point, and Blake took his time about replying.

'Then, to satisfy you, I am engaged to Eleanor. I can't see why there should be any doubt about it.'

'She told us you had disagreed quite violently with her intention of coming to see me.'

'As to that, yes, I did tell her she was being a little fool.' He laughed, a little awkwardly. 'But, damn it all, you can't quarrel with a girl for being soft-hearted.'

'No, I see. Tell me about the weekend of the crime.'

'I don't know that there's anything to tell.' He paused a moment, thinking about it. 'Eleanor was spending the weekend at the DeLisles' – her parents too, of course – so I suppose it seemed natural to Mrs. DeLisle to ask me to dinner on the Saturday.'

'Did you have any previous acquaintance with the DeLisles?'

'No.'

'You hadn't even heard of the firm DeLisle Brothers?'

'Well, yes, they had a robbery about three years ago. From the shop.'

'Did you cover the case?'

'Yes. I met George DeLisle then, but not his brother.'

'Was the thief ever found?'

'I don't think so. Certainly not while I was still interested in the matter.'

'I hope they were well insured.'

'I can't say about that.'

'Did Mrs. DeLisle tell you the occasion for the dinner party?'

'No, but Eleanor did. She was all excited about seeing the jewellery; I suppose any woman would be.'

'Was Lady Bowling excited?'

'Why should you think I'd know a thing like that?'

'I understood – ' That sentence had nowhere it could go, he let it trail beguilingly.

'Yes, she did mention it to me, that the party was for her and old man Bowling really. I didn't take much interest, and I don't remember that she seemed particularly excited.'

'So Mrs. DeLisle telephoned you?'

'On the Thursday afternoon. She said she'd been trying to get me all day, but I'd been out on assignment.'

'Tell me something about the people concerned. As I understand it, the Wyatts were already acquainted with the DeLisles, and also with the Bowlings.'

'That's right. I believe the Wyatts and the Bowlings are quite close friends.'

'What did you think of the DeLisles when you made their acquaintance?'

'I was interested because it was an odd household . . . man and his wife, and bachelor brother. But it seemed to work very well.'

'You know rather more of the Wyatts, I suppose, considering your engagement to their daughter.'

'Well, yes. Nothing that could interest you.'

'Did Mrs. Wyatt seem excited too, by the jewellery?'

'All the women were more . . . well, fascinated by it, I suppose, than the men were. Which to me seems natural.'

'Except Sir Leonard Bowling?'

'He was buying the stuff, wasn't he? Or thinking about it. I should think that was a pretty good reason myself for taking an interest.'

'It seems strange that during the intervening months he has made no attempt to find another source of supply.'

'Hasn't he? I wouldn't know about that, but I don't imagine these things grow on trees, do you?'

'I just thought . . . but, as you are about to point out, Mr. Blake, that has nothing to do with me. How well do you know the Bowlings?'

'I've met them socially a few times . . . a very casual acquaintanceship. Of course, Sir Leonard is, in a sense, my employer, but we don't see much of him at the paper. Occasionally an edict comes down from on high, that's about all.'

'I see. You wouldn't know anything about their relationship to each other then?'

'No, I wouldn't!'

There was a danger signal there, Geoffrey thought,

if ever he saw one, but Antony went on regardless. 'Or about his personal finances?'

Laurence Blake dealt with that by getting on his dignity. 'Really, Mr. Maitland, I fail to see – '

'Grant for a moment that I'm fishing in the dark. Would you answer if you thought it a reasonable question?'

'I couldn't. Considering the amount of outlay he was proposing on jewellery I imagine his financial position is rather to be envied than otherwise.'

'You know Lady Bowling tried to conceal the fact that she intended to go downstairs again after the ladies had retired for the night?'

The abrupt question took Blake by surprise, there was no doubt about that. He spluttered over his answer, made several false starts, and then said, still indignant, 'I know you gave her a bad time in court over a point that couldn't have the slightest significance.'

'That, after all, is a matter of opinion.'

Blake was on his feet. 'I don't like questions about my friends,' he said. And then, with an obvious attempt at a more amiable tone, 'We'll call it a day, shall we?'

Geoffrey Horton, who was no more happy than he had been at yesterday's interviews, was up in a trice. Antony followed his example more slowly. 'The most casual acquaintance,' he said thoughtfully. 'That was what you said, wasn't it?'

'It was, and it's true. All the same – '

'It seems a pity to leave matters here.'

'What else, in God's name, can you want from me?'

Antony smiled; this time there seemed to be some genuine amusement in it. 'Mr. Horton would certainly have preferred me to approach the subject more tactfully,' he said, 'but I could bear to know what you did after you left the DeLisles' home that night.'

'I came back here. What would you expect?' He

walked over to the door and flung it open, and said with quite unnatural calm, 'And that, Mr. Maitland, is the final straw. I don't need to provide an alibi, to you or anybody else.'

Antony began to move across the room in a leisurely way that reminded Geoffrey irresistibly of Sir Nicholas. 'It would be nice, even so, if you could prove that,' he said gently.

They were eye to eye in the doorway now, and for a moment it was touch and go, Geoffrey thought, whether Blake would hit him. It was just like Antony to provoke a situation like this, when he knew perfectly well he couldn't hold his own owing to his injured shoulder. But though Blake's left hand clenched ominously, he did not relax his hold on the door knob with his right. 'I always understood Chief Inspector Sykes was a friend of yours,' he said, with a mocking inflection in his voice. 'Why don't you ask him?'

'He's a prosecution witness. I can't approach him in this case.'

'How unfortunate for you. Well, I shouldn't like you to lose any sleep over the matter, so I'll tell you. I live alone, and I met nobody on the journey.'

'Thank you.'

'And now, get out!'

'We're on our way. Come along, Geoffrey,' he added, as though there was any doubt that Horton would be close on his heels. A moment later the door of the flat closed with a decisive snap behind them.

Their next appointment was in Pinner, so there was plenty of time for conversation on the way, which on Geoffrey's part was inclined to be querulous. Antony, however, had no intention of indulging him by listening overlong to his recriminations, saying only, 'It's all very terrible, I agree, but I don't see what else I could have done in the circumstances, do you?' And then, when Horton's indignation brought him temporarily to silence, 'Do you realise, this man Thurlow is very much of an unknown quantity still? Nobody seems to have had anything to say about him.'

'That,' said Geoffrey, not without a certain malicious satisfaction, 'must be because you haven't asked the right questions.'

'Very likely. But don't you think that's odd in itself?'

Geoffrey gave the appearance of thinking this over. 'No,' he said at last. Antony laughed.

'It's just that I wonder what we're going to find,' he said.

What they found was a small, modern house, set in a beautifully kept garden, which even at this sombre time of year contrived to look attractive. They were admitted by a tall, pale, bespectacled man who acknowledged cautiously – as though the fact might somehow be used against him – that he was Godfrey Thurlow. And after the bland modernity of the exterior, the interior was a surprise. The place was filled – almost literally – with antiques, which from their looks alone must be worth a lot of money. There was no attempt at establishing a period, everything was jumbled together, from an ancient bureau that had a French look about it, to an elegantly upholstered and undeniably Victorian sofa, on which Geoffrey took refuge when their host said, 'Sit down, sit down,' and waved his hand vaguely, as being probably the least uncomfortable thing in the room. Antony had to content himself with a large oaken chair, with a hard wooden seat and a knobbly wooden back, in which he was acutely uncomfortable. He wondered, in passing, whether Thurlow found this the sort of room he could relax in, or whether there was another, snugger room tucked away in the house to which policy, or sheer sadism, had forbidden him to take his visitors. If it were the former he was likely to get his way; nobody would stay here a moment beyond what was necessary.

For once he allowed Horton to explain their errand, which he did with admirable terseness. Thurlow looked vaguely surprised, but made no comment except to say, looking from one of them to the other, that he would be glad to do anything he could to help. Antony pounced on the statement as though a witness in court had made a dangerous admission.

'You don't feel any animus against Malcolm Harte, then?'

'No, why should I? I saw him for a few hours one evening, in company with a number of other people. He may even be innocent, for all I know.'

'You'd agree though – wouldn't you? – that the guilty party is probably one of the people who were present that evening.'

'I really haven't given the matter very much thought.'

'A thief without inside knowledge would have gone to the shop, rather than to the DeLisles' home.'

'Yes, that is an interesting point of view.' He sounded as though the idea had never occurred to him before. 'Well, well, Eleanor assures me that the police have made a mistake.' He glanced at Geoffrey, and then let his eyes rest reflectively on Antony's face. 'Who would you put in young Harte's place, Mr. Maitland?'

'I'm . . . fishing in the dark,' said Antony, making use of the phrase he had used before.

'I wonder how I can help you.'

'First, by telling me all you can about the people who were at the DeLisles' that night.'

'But of them all I only knew Eleanor,' Thurlow protested. 'And her parents, a little. I dined with them once, when she first came to work for me.'

'Tell me about Eleanor, then.'

'A good girl, with a sensitive appreciation of the finer things of life.'

'That requires some definition,' said Antony, smiling.

'Music . . . art . . . the ballet . . . antiques in general; all the things she came into daily contact with at the Gallery.'

'Would you put her down as a good judge of character?'

It was Thurlow's turn to smile. Something about the question amused him. 'On the whole, I think not,' he said.

'Now, why – ?'

'I'm sorry, Mr. Maitland. I can give you no reason for that opinion.'

'I wonder if it has anything to do with your assessment of her father's character.'

Thurlow shook his head at him; not, he thought, altogether in negation, but rather in denial of the question's validity. 'Well, perhaps that wasn't fair,' Antony conceded. 'You didn't know the DeLisles, then, until Mrs. DeLisle telephoned you?'

'By reputation only. Henry DeLisle is known as a fine artist.'

'You don't agree?'

'Not entirely. But I shouldn't say that, it is a matter of one's personal taste really. His work is too modern for me.'

'Then you preferred the jewellery as it was to the new designs that were shown to you.'

'A thousand times!' For the first time he showed something approaching animation. 'In my mind, Mr. Maitland, it was nothing short of criminal to propose to break up those fine pieces.'

'I see. You must have been surprised to hear from Mrs. DeLisle.'

'Perhaps a little. But Eleanor had mentioned to me

123

what was proposed, and I gathered she had spoken to Mrs. DeLisle about me. I am not particularly interested in parties, Mr. Maitland, but the opportunity of seeing the DeLisle collection – '

'You'd heard of it, then?'

'Certainly. There was no secret about it, or that he wanted the pieces for Sir Leonard Bowling. In fact, for one particular pendant I had bid against him, but unsuccessfully, I'm afraid. The economics of a place like mine don't permit over-spending on one particular item, unless you have an assured market for it.'

Again Antony turned the subject slightly, just when Geoffrey thought he should be getting interested in what was being said. 'Still, it wasn't an unpleasant party, as such things go.'

'By no means. Mrs. DeLisle is a charming woman, an excellent hostess, and if the guests weren't altogether congenial – '

'Wait a bit! You mean there was some unpleasantness?'

'Nothing like that. Just a slight feeling of tension – which I may well have been imagining – between Sir Leonard and the young man Blake, whom I understand is employed by him.'

'Could you possibly be any more definite than that?'

'I'm afraid not. It was a fleeting impression only.'

'Anything else of a similar nature?'

'No, unless . . . the two girls. I had always heard Eleanor speak of Mary Reynolds as a friend, but they didn't seem friendly that evening.'

'Did anyone seem to take a particular interest in the jewellery?'

'I was engrossed myself. I'm afraid I didn't notice.'

'Then, when you left, Mr. Thurlow. How did that come about?'

'I'm afraid I don't understand you.'

'You and Blake left together, didn't you? Was that at his suggestion, or yours?'

'I believe I was the first to mention leaving. The show was over . . . this sounds ungrateful, Mr. Maitland, but as I told you I am not fond of social gatherings.'

'And Blake came too?'

'Like me, he wasn't a friend of the family. I suppose it seemed an appropriate moment for the party to break up.'

'Yes, I see. How did you get home?'

'I had my car. The journey across town – '

'And Blake?'

'By car also. He had to back out into the road before I could move.'

'You came straight home?'

'Yes.'

'Is there anyone who can confirm that?'

'I'm afraid not.'

Antony got to his feet. 'You take the question very calmly,' he said.

'Why not? I have been anticipating it ever since Mr. Horton phoned me.' He was still maddeningly calm. Antony laughed, and they took their leave.

Geoffrey insisted on taking him all the way back to Kempenfeldt Square, though it was out of his way, but he wouldn't stop for tea. Antony went upstairs to find, as he had expected, Sir Nicholas ensconced in his favourite arm-chair, eating hot buttered toast. Jenny had the tea-tray beside her, but at the moment both their cups were full, and she was looking relaxed and peaceful.

'What's happened to Meg and Roger?' Antony asked, as he made for the fire.

Jenny bestirred herself. 'Meg's got a cold,' she said.

'Roger phoned. I don't suppose it's anything much, but it would be dreadful if she lost her voice.'

'I expect it's just Roger making a fuss,' said Antony heartlessly. He accepted a cup of tea, and placed it behind him on the mantelpiece.

'That seems rather a harsh judgment, surely,' said Sir Nicholas. 'It would be kinder to assume that he didn't want to run the risk of passing on the infection to us.'

'No, because it's funny about Roger. His idea of pleasure is to put up with any extreme of heat or cold, or other discomfort, on that yacht of his, but where Meg's concerned he's like a hen with one chick.'

'I find that an admirable trait,' said Sir Nicholas. Antony grinned at him.

'So do I really.' He took a plate from the tray, helped himself to three scones and a piece of fruit cake, and went back to his place with his back to, but a little to one side of the fire.

'Did you have a – a profitable afternoon?' Jenny asked.

'Not particularly.'

'You're still on this wild goose chase of yours,' said Sir Nicholas in an accusatory tone.

'For once, Uncle Nick, that's a pretty good description. I've got a sort of an idea – '

'Come now! You either have an idea or you haven't.'

'Well then, I've got an idea, but it's a pretty wild one.'

'Has anything transpired that will be of use to the defence?' Sir Nicholas demanded.

'Not a thing.'

'Are you going to call any of these people you have been seeing this weekend?'

'Well – ' He drew out the word doubtfully.

'You say there's nothing – '

'No, but I've asked Geoffrey to subpoena the lot of them, just in case Father William comes up with something. You see, I think – '

'Eleanor Wyatt was here just after lunch,' said Jenny, as he let that sentence trail into silence. If she was meaning to create a diversion she was successful; Sir Nicholas picked up his cup and looked at her severely over its rim.

'You didn't tell me that.' And at the same moment Antony asked eagerly,

'Was there anything – ?'

'She wanted to see you. I'm sorry, Uncle Nick, but I didn't want to have to go through it twice. So, of course, when Gibbs told me I asked her to come up here, and if there'd been anything important, Antony, I'd have kept her here somehow until you came. But I think it was just curiosity . . . no, I shouldn't say that, she's *anxious* about Malcolm Harte.'

'Yes, I see.'

'You wouldn't have wanted to see her, just for that?' asked Jenny, a little anxious herself.

'No, I'm sure you were much kinder to her than I should have been.' He finished his tea, and held out his cup for a refill. 'And Eleanor, in spite of having started the whole thing, is the last person I'd expect to have anything helpful to say.'

'She did tell me one thing,' said Jenny, concentrating on getting the last drop out of a teapot that felt suspiciously empty, 'but it wasn't helpful, just interesting.'

'Thank you. If you're trying to tantalise me, love – '

'No, of course not. She told me her engagement to Laurence Blake is on again.'

'I gathered as much from him. He said, "you can't blame a girl for being kind-hearted".'

'That sounds a bit – a bit condescending to me,' said

Jenny thoughtfully. 'Still, of course, I'm glad for Eleanor's sake. She seems a very nice girl.'

'Did she seem pleased with the development?'

'Oh, yes, I think so. But it was hard to tell, because at the same time she's so worried about Malcolm Harte.'

'If that is a sample of the information you have gained this weekend,' said Sir Nicholas crushingly, 'I'm not surprised you feel that you have accomplished very little. Still, if it has persuaded you that the only way to treat the case is on its merits, I suppose no harm has been done.'

'It hasn't any merits, Uncle Nick, that's the trouble. And unless we call Bowling, and Wyatt, and the others – '

'Which on your own showing isn't likely.'

' – we've only one witness, Malcolm Harte, denying everything. And that's it.'

'Then you must concentrate a little on your opening and closing addresses, my dear boy,' said Sir Nicholas, not without malice. 'I'm sure, with your powers of persuasion – '

Antony and Jenny exchanged a despairing glance, and started, simultaneously, to try to change the subject.

There was no word from Father William that evening.

MONDAY, the third day

Detective Chief Inspector Sykes was a placid man, who took things very much as they came. He was square-built, dark, with a comfortable, country look about him, even here in court where he was very conscious of the proprieties. The seventh juror, looking at him, thought you might have taken him for a farmer . . . a prosperous farmer, well contented with his lot.

The weekend break had been a very welcome one. The seventh juror, who sat immediately behind the foreman, was conscious of boredom, even more so than before the recess. This was a confirmation of all the things Garfield had said in his opening statement, a repetition of evidence already given by the expert witnesses. He was inclined to approve of Sykes, as being what he thought of as a good, old-fashioned policeman, but that didn't mean to say that he must hang on his every word. Maitland, when his turn came, would say that the evidence was circumstantial; it didn't take much brain to work that out. For himself, it was sufficient. There were always things you knew, but couldn't prove. Where would he be if he had to find cut-and-dried evidence against Travers, for instance? But Travers was a thief, he knew that as well as if he'd got a written confession; as well as being an aggravating boy, constantly lost in a dream, but with a disconcerting habit of coming up with the correct answer to a question when he seemed to be least attending.

The seventh juror was a big man, flabbily fat, with shaggy grey hair, a rumpled suit, and ash on his lapels from the cigarette he had enjoyed just before coming into court. By profession he was a schoolmaster, teaching English and History to the upper forms at one of the comprehensive schools. That was where he ought to be now, he'd heard enough of this case to convince him of the guilt of the accused. You got a sixth sense about that kind of thing after a few years dealing all the time with one kind of villainy or another on the part of the young. Come to think of it, you could very well compare his feeling about this case with the feeling he had about Travers. Absolute certainty, even if the evidence was circumstantial. Or perhaps, if he were to be completely honest with himself, not even circumstantial in Travers's case.

It was always unpleasant when you got an outbreak of stealing in a school. The boys had been warned, of course, not to leave money in their lockers, but there were still some who would do it, preferring to keep their trousers' pockets for the important miscellany that seemed to be essential to their comfort

. . . *penknives, pieces of string, and the rest. Someone had been using a penknife of his own, cleverly enough to leave no obvious trace until the owner of the locker came along with his key. He'd thought of Travers immediately, he had a shifty look about him at the best of times.*

No good going to the headmaster. He and Maitland would make a good pair, demanding proof where certainty already existed. But a word to Bolton would do the trick all right; he was a good type of boy, solid, dependable, not questioning everything that was told him. And not one to keep his mouth shut about a thing like this. There'd been a good deal of indignation in the school about what was happening, Travers wouldn't be getting away with it so easily any longer. You might say it was even doing him a favour, might cure him of the desire to steal for life. But he'd have liked to be in a position to see the result of that quiet word, see how quickly the news spread, see how quickly Travers became an outcast. Teaching was a boring job, anything was welcome to break the monotony; and here he was, up to his neck in something even more boring. He prided himself on being a good judge of character, and he wouldn't have trusted this fellow Harte an inch, not an inch, even if he'd met him in the most ordinary of circumstances.

But Counsel for the Prosecution, who'd been getting everything his own way, was sitting down now, looking – for all his austerity of countenance – a little like the cat who has swallowed the cream. It might be amusing, though not instructive, to see what his opponent made of the witness. He'd have his work cut out to get a rise out of the Chief Inspector, that was for certain . . .

But Maitland wasn't sure that he wanted to do that. Always supposing that it was possible with so placid a man as Sykes. He got to his feet in a leisurely way, but that was in unconscious imitation of his uncle, not out of any idea of intimidating the witness. 'You will admit, Chief Inspector, that this case, as my friend has so ably

130

outlined it for us, remains a circumstantial one.'

Almost any other police officer would have pointed out, with truth, that this was only too often the case, particularly with a murder charge. Sykes contented himself with saying, 'Yes,' and contrived to look intelligently interested in what the next question would be; rather, thought Maitland a little savagely to himself, as though he was wondering in what way counsel would next make a fool of himself.

'The morning-room window *was* found open on the morning after the crime?'

'It was.'

'I am well aware of your explanation for that: that my client had passed out the jewellery to an accomplice. But don't you think it equally likely that some intruder, the real culprit, came and went that way.'

Sykes considered this before answering. 'In all the circumstances, no, Mr. Maitland, I do not.'

Well, that was only to be expected. 'Your enquiries have turned up no trace of the jewellery, I believe.'

'I regret to say that is so.'

'And there is nothing, absolutely nothing to suggest that George DeLisle was killed while Mr. Harte was with him, rather than at some later time?'

But that was too much for Garfield. 'My lord!' he said. 'My learned friend should have asked that question of the medical witnesses.' (He had done, of course, but would the jury remember that?) 'It is not within the competence of this witness – '

Mr. Justice Conroy was nodding his agreement. Maitland sighed, and patiently began to go through the prosecution's contentions, one by one, from the beginning. But there was no shaking Sykes, and when he was done Garfield did not consider it worth while to re-examine.

THE CASE FOR THE DEFENCE

MONDAY, the third day (continued)

It all took time, but even so Maitland was able to make his brief opening remarks – the case for the prosecution being concluded – before the luncheon recess. He rushed his companions through lunch, and sent Geoffrey Horton down to see their client before the court reconvened. Because it was time for Malcolm Harte's evidence now, and he was suddenly, unexpectedly nervous as to what sort of a showing that young man would make.

To begin with he told his story well, and with very little prompting. Yes, he thought it was fair to say that he had hoped Mrs. DeLisle would invite him for the weekend, along with Mary Reynolds, staying in the same house they would surely have some chance of seeing each other, and that had been his only motive in wanting to go to Wimbledon. He knew the jewellery well, of course; he had the keys to the strong-room at the shop, as well as to the display cases, could have helped himself at any time.

'Was it usual for you to travel with so much jewellery in your possession?'

'Not really. Well, I'd never had to go to the Wimbledon house before, but quite frequently a client staying in a hotel will want to see a selection . . . of rings, for instance. I usually take a cab.'

'Did you travel by taxi to Wimbledon on the thirteenth June?'

'Yes.'

'And Miss Reynolds accompanied you?'

'She did. And I think Mr. Henry was right, you know, we were out of place in that party. But it was kind of Mrs. DeLisle to ask us.'

'You have had the opportunity of hearing the evidence of the prosecution witnesses, Mr. Harte. Is there any point about the events of that day on which you would like to correct them?'

'Not really. Of course, I didn't know Lady Bowling was on the stairs behind me when I went down to the study.'

'Then we will come straight away to what happened in the evening . . . to the showing of the jewellery, to be specific. You didn't take much interest in that.'

'No, because of course I knew what was there by heart already. So did Mary; I mean, she'd seen all the pieces, although not as often as I had. It was the first chance we'd had of a word together since we were out in the afternoon, because dinner was very formal and we weren't sitting together. So we went over to the window, a little withdrawn from the others. Mind you, I could quite understand *their* interest, there were some very lovely stones.'

You never could tell until you got them in the box. A few minutes ago Maitland would have taken a small bet that Harte would prove a poor witness, and here he was, casual, almost relaxed. There could be no doubt he was creating a good impression. Perhaps, after all . . .

'Now we are coming to the crux of the matter, Mr. Harte, and I want you to be very careful of your answers, because my learned friend, Mr. Garfield, will be particularly interested in what you have to say. At what time did the showing of the jewellery finish, and what happened after that?'

'I suppose it was about ten-thirty. I didn't look at my watch until later on. Mr. George broke up the party, saying he'd put the jewellery away and then write some letters. Mr. Thurlow and Mr. Blake left soon after that, and when Lady Bowling suggested retiring I was quite glad to do so along with the ladies. I'd have been out of place in the small group that was left behind.'

'Yes, that is very clear. But what I want you to explain to us, Mr. Harte, is why you decided to come downstairs again.'

'It was on an impulse – '

'You didn't, for instance – my friend will certainly suggest this to you – you didn't go upstairs in the first place purely to create the impression that you had gone to bed?'

'No. It was only when I got to my room that it occurred to me that it would be a good opportunity to see Mr. George alone.'

'Why did you wish to do so?'

'It was only . . . well, you see, our wedding plans were made and the arrangements for the honeymoon, and then he said that perhaps I'd have to put off my holiday after all.' And for the first time he sounded hesitant, and for the first time since his client went into the witness box Maitland felt a qualm. All the same . . .

'We must have this quite clear, Mr. Harte,' he said. 'Mr. George DeLisle dealt, among other things, with matters of personnel.'

'That's right.' That was said almost eagerly, too eagerly for Maitland's taste. 'He spoke to me about it on Friday afternoon,' the prisoner went on, 'and, of course, I protested. But he took me by surprise, I hadn't time to – to marshal my arguments, so I thought if I could have a word with him quietly, where we weren't likely to be interrupted, I could make him see – '

'Had you spoken to Miss Reynolds about this possible change of plan?' asked Maitland, when it became obvious that the witness wasn't going to go on unprompted.

'No, I knew . . . I should say I *thought* she'd be disappointed. I was going to be quite sure of my facts, make sure we really had to change our arrangements, before I spoke to her.'

'So you decided to go down and see Mr. George DeLisle.'

'Yes, I thought perhaps at home, and with the sale almost certain to go through . . . well, I thought perhaps he'd be a bit more reasonable. And here I *can* tell you the time,' Malcolm added in a pleased tone. (Or was he only pleased that a difficult point in his testimony had been passed?) 'I had only just got to my room, and it was just turned ten-forty – say about eighteen minutes to. And I thought, if I was going to do it I'd get it over with. And I went straight down.'

'You knew where the study was?'

'Yes, I had taken the jewellery there to Mr. George when we first arrived that afternoon.'

'It may be as well at this point to ask you, are you familiar with the lay-out of the Wimbledon house?'

'I had never been there before.'

'So downstairs you were only familiar with – ?'

'The drawing-room, the dining-room, the study.'

'You did not, for instance, know where the morning-room was?'

'No.'

'Tell us then, Mr. Harte – '

'I went straight to the study door and knocked, and waited till I heard him say, "Come in". Mr. George was sitting at the desk – '

'What was he doing? Was he writing the letters he spoke of?'

'No, he had the new designs spread out in front of him, looking them over. And the case in which I had brought the jewellery from the shop was on the corner of the desk.'

'What happened then?'

Malcolm was speaking slowly now, picking his words 'He looked up, frowning, didn't seem pleased by the interruption. But when I asked him about my holiday he was – was much more reasonable than he had been before. He quite readily agreed that I could take it as arranged, and we spent a few minutes talking about arrangements for my absence.'

'And then – ?'

'He said, "Since you're here you may as well make yourself useful". And when I asked, How? he told me to put away the jewel cases in the safe.'

'Let us be quite clear about this. The jewel cases were in the attaché case in which you had originally brought them to Wimbledon?'

'That's right. It was easier to carry them about the house in that, I suppose, but I took them out – I supposed that was what he meant me to do – and stacked them in the safe, which was open, and left the attaché case standing by the desk.

'Was there anything else in the safe?'

'Not a thing.'

'And when the jewel cases were safely bestowed – ?'

'I looked at Mr. George to see if he wanted me to close the safe, but he shook his head and said, "Leave it for the time". So I just pushed it closed without spinning the dial and said, "Good night", and went back upstairs.'

'But not straight to your room.'

'No. I thought I might as well have a last word with Mary – with Miss Reynolds. So I went to her room – '

'You knew which one it was?'

'We all went upstairs together. Remember?'

'Miss Reynolds has told us that you left her again at "not quite eleven".'

'Well, I don't think I was in the study more than ten

minutes at the most, and Mary bundled me out of her room so quickly, I should think five to would be nearer.'

'There is something else in Miss Reynolds's evidence that I think I should ask you to explain. She said you seemed excited, almost elated when she saw you.'

'That's easily explained.' (If that were so, why did he look so uneasy? Perhaps not such a good witness after all.) 'I'd have told her if she'd given me half a chance. You see, I'd almost made up my mind to having to postpone the wedding, or perhaps getting married when we intended but not having a honeymoon until later. So when everything turned out to be all right . . . well, naturally I was pleased about it.'

'Another point has been raised, about your honeymoon arrangements. It is suggested that there was some sinister significance in the choice of Amsterdam as a place to visit. Perhaps you can clarify that for us.'

'Mary wanted to see Paris, so we were starting from there. We had a very careful itinerary worked out, and that was where I reckoned we'd be at the end of a fortnight. And, you know, if I'd really intended to dispose of my ill-gotten gains there – ' (Never volunteer anything, thought Maitland despairingly. I must have told him that a dozen times.) ' – I'd have arranged to go there first, not at the end of a touring holiday.'

'Precisely.' (All he could do now was to sound pleased with the statement.) 'And now, Mr. Harte, there are one or two points on which perhaps the jury may not be quite clear . . . '

More repetition. You'd think we were a group of morons, the way they repeat themselves. But the man told his story well, you might almost be inclined to believe him. Of course, the motive was understandable, his fingerprints on the safe damning, but he had explained those. Could you believe him, with so much at stake? That was another matter, it would be interesting to see what his fellow-jurors thought about it in due course. If ever the trial ended . . .

There were so many more interesting things to consider, thought the eighth juror, than the fate of the pale man who was now in the witness box. The question of Beryl, for instance. He'd never liked the child from the first time he saw her, a scrawny little thing, standing close to her mother as if in some way she was afraid of him. A girl of fourteen, nearly sixteen now.

Ruth told him afterwards that she'd explained things as gently as she could . . . that she was lonely, needed the companionship of a husband . . . that he would be like a new father to her. Perhaps it was instinct, they say dogs and children . . . but the fact remained that she had shrunk from him from the first, almost as if he had offered her physical violence. Which wasn't his way.

He'd suggested to Ruth that very evening that Beryl might be happier in a boarding-school, but she wouldn't hear of it. 'Poor child, she's so confused now, and upset, it would only make her think we didn't want her.' Well, there were more subtle ways of getting what he wanted. It was being a long grind, longer than he had expected, but now, for the first time . . .

He'd been the soul of patience with Beryl's moods, whenever Ruth was present. Perhaps the girl would have come to accept him in time, but that wasn't what he wanted. He wasn't sharing Ruth with anyone. But in the end it proved to be so easy, Beryl was so dreadfully insecure by this time. The day she'd come home from school all starry-eyed over being given the part of Audrey in the school production of As you like it. 'They don't want you to act, my dear,' he'd said to her when he got her alone. 'Just be yourself, that's all they expect of you.' It had taken her a minute to get it, and when she did there was enough truth in the gibe to make her burst into tears. That time she had run to Ruth with the story, and Ruth − bless her − had sided with him as soon as she heard his denials. 'You must get over being so jealous, darling, and never, never, never make up such *a wicked story about your step-father again.' After that it had been easy . . . take every opportunity of undermining the girl's self-confidence, and know that she'd die rather than tell Ruth what was going on.*

It had had its effect on her, of course. And now, this last weekend, for the first time Ruth had been willing to discuss a boarding-school. 'One where they know how to deal with difficult children, because I'm at my wits' end.' By the time the trial was over – and perhaps before that, at this rate – the whole thing would be settled.

But meanwhile there was Maitland sitting down, and Garfield coming slowly to his feet. The prisoner, still in the witness box, was looking . . . well, more rattled than anything else. So far he had made a good showing, but by the time Garfield had finished with him the overall picture might be different . . .

Garfield had evidently decided to plunge, without preliminaries, *in medias res.* 'You say you could have helped yourself at any time to items from the strong-room or the display cases at the shop. If you had done that, would not the theft have been easily traceable to you?'

'No more easily than the theft at Wimbledon – which I did not commit – was put down to my doing.'

'But you were seen going into the study. I'm sure it was no part of your plan to admit that you had been there.'

'My lord!' said Maitland, this time in genuine indignation. Conroy turned weary eyes on Counsel for the Prosecution.

'Mr. Garfield, I must remind you that the verdict is not yet in. The jury will disregard that remark.'

'As your lordship pleases.' Garfield, thought Maitland, is in one of his crusading moods. An anti-immorality crusade, that's it! I shouldn't have harped on the fact that Harte went to the Reynolds girl's room at the highly irregular hour of ten-fifty, or whenever it was. It's typical of my learned adversary that he can be genuinely shocked by such a half-hearted attempt at seduction. Only I didn't have any choice, after she'd blurted out that Harte looked elated. In any event, there's nothing to be done about it now.

'You planned to take your honeymoon in Europe,' Garfield was continuing. 'Had you ever been abroad before?'

'No.'

'Not to Amsterdam, then?'

'No.'

'Paris I can understand, but why Amsterdam in particular?'

'I thought I had explained that when we worked out our route that seemed the logical place to finish up.'

'Still, there is the fact that you are familiar with some dealers there.'

'Certainly. But I don't think Mr. Henry DeLisle will care for the implication that his contacts there are a bunch of crooks.'

It wasn't wise to be pert with Garfield, though Maitland conceded the temptation. Oh, well, the fellow was on his own now, at least unless any obvious cause for an objection arose. With a judge like Conroy it wasn't safe to intervene too often frivolously, he might be in need of a little latitude himself later on.

Garfield was frowning his displeasure. 'That was not my intention, as I think you very well know,' he said heavily. 'We will turn to another point, and perhaps if you see any humour in this you will be wise enough to keep that fact to yourself. You say you had never before been to the DeLisles' house at Wimbledon.'

'Yes. I mean, that was the first time, that day.'

'Mr. Henry DeLisle has told us that you gave the

jewellery to him, and that he himself took it to the study. That does not quite agree with your statement that you went to the study yourself at that time.'

'Yes, it does, because Mr. Henry was in the hall when we arrived. I gave him the case, but accompanied him to the study to see the jewellery safely disposed.'

'Why did you do that, Mr. Harte? It hardly seems necessary – '

'Curiosity, I suppose. As I said, I had never been to the house before.'

'Do you remember how many doors there are leading out of the hall, besides the front door?'

'No.'

'There are six. Perhaps your lordship will be good enough to refer to the plan, and the members of the jury too,' Garfield invited. 'Two doors on each side of the hall,' he went on, addressing the prisoner again, 'and a service door and the door to the downstairs cloakroom at the back. Of the four doors in the main body of the hall, you have admitted to knowing where three of them lead . . . to the drawing-room, the dining-room, and the study. That is correct, is it not?'

'Yes.'

'Then I do not think it would be difficult to work out the fact that the remaining door led to the morning-room.'

'If I'd known there was a morning-room. I didn't.'

'To some room, then, that wasn't in general use.'

'I suppose you're right, but I don't see why – '

'Don't you, Mr. Harte?' That was said mockingly, and Maitland came to his feet in a hurry before his opponent could go on.

'My friend will have plenty of opportunity to address the jury later, my lord. This is not the time – '

'Yes, Mr. Maitland, the point is taken. I think you must refrain from comment at this juncture, Mr. Garfield.'

'Very well, my lord. You have admitted doing your best, Mr. Harte, to influence Mrs. DeLisle into inviting you to Wimbledon that weekend.'

'Yes, I – '

'And to include Miss Reynolds in the invitation?'

'Well, that was the whole point of it.'

'I have no doubt that is what you wish us to think. You will agree, however, that this did not give you much opportunity of being alone together.'

'Not so much as I had hoped.'

'Until after the majority of the party had retired to bed.'

'I don't quite know what you mean by that.'

'You are telling us, Mr. Harte, that your purpose in obtaining the invitation was to see Miss Reynolds alone; it is obvious that the only opportunity to do this was to go to her bedroom at night.'

'Well – '

'Which you did.'

'Yes.'

'In spite of the fact that you must have known perfectly well that Miss Reynolds is a young lady of principle, who would be deeply shocked by the suggestion of pre-marital intercourse.'

'Yes, I knew that.'

'Then I put it to you that your ostensible reason for obtaining the invitation falls to the ground. If you could not expect Miss Reynolds to fall in with your plan, I suggest that it was never made at all. I suggest that you went to Wimbledon because you knew the jewellery would be more vulnerable there, that a burglary would be more likely, that you would not be so easily suspected – '

'You can suggest what you like. It doesn't make it true.'

'Tell me then, did you tell the police straight away

that you had been downstairs again, and actually in the study?'

'No.'

'When did you tell them?'

'Not until after Lady Bowling told them about seeing me. And I think you can guess the reason for that.'

'I am not here to play guessing games,' said Garfield austerely.

'Well, if you want it spelled out, I thought it would make them suspect me, and it did.'

'It is not difficult to see why.' He broke off there; he might have been framing his next question carefully, but more likely, Maitland thought, the pause was purely for effect. 'You agree with the prosecution witnesses,' Garfield went on after a moment, 'about the time the showing of the jewellery ended.'

'I don't see anything particularly incriminating about that,' Malcolm retorted. I warned him, thought Maitland again; but unwise as his client's tone might be, at least he was keeping his end up, and perhaps that was something to be thankful for.

'Mr. George DeLisle was the first to leave the drawing-room, taking the jewellery with him, and saying he was going to stay in the study and write some letters. Is that correct?'

'Quite correct.'

'I suggest to you that it was then that the idea first occurred to you that here was your opportunity of getting hold of the jewellery before it was locked away in the safe.'

'I wish you would make up your mind about things,' Malcolm grumbled. 'Am I supposed to have known the combination of the safe, or not?'

'Mr. Harte.' The judge was leaning forward. 'You are here to answer counsel's questions. You will do yourself no good – '

'Thank you, my lord.' Malcolm turned a little to face the bench; it seemed likely that he was glad to get away for the moment from Garfield's attack. 'But it does seem to me – '

'No good at all, Mr. Harte,' said Conroy, shaking his head. 'You may continue, Mr. Garfield.'

'His lordship has directed you to answer my question,' Garfield said.

'I'm afraid I've forgotten what it was.'

'I suggested to you that when you heard that Mr. George DeLisle was going to be alone in the study it struck you as a good opportunity of getting hold of the jewellery before it was locked in the safe.'

'I never thought that at any time. I thought I made that clear. I *did* want to talk to him, but it only occurred to me later that this would be a good opportunity.'

'So you went down to the study, had an entirely amicable conversation with Mr. George DeLisle about the plans for your holiday – ' Garfield's tone was heavily sarcastic, and Malcolm interrupted him rather hurriedly.

'That's right.'

' – which nobody else, apparently, knew to be in jeopardy.'

'I don't know why he never told Mr. Henry, but I've already explained why I didn't want to tell Mary until I was sure.'

'And conveniently – you will admit it was convenient, Mr. Harte – Mr. DeLisle asked you to put the jewel cases away in the safe.'

'I don't quite see why you call it convenient.'

'Because it explains so neatly why your fingerprints were found on the cases, and on the door of the safe.' He paused there, but the witness did not try to interrupt him again. 'I put it to you then,' he went on, speaking slowly now, every word carrying its weight, 'that the opportunity was too much for you. There was the piece of amethyst conveniently to hand, there was the safe, conveniently open, and everybody – so far as you knew – thought that you had retired to bed.'

'That just isn't true.'

'So you tell us, Mr. Harte, so you tell us. You may even be telling the truth when you say that the jewel cases were still in the attaché case in which you brought them to Wimbledon. In that event, your task was even simpler. You had told your accomplice to watch the house, to wait until he saw you open a window – '

'May I remind the court, my lord,' said Maitland, coming to his feet, 'that this accomplice is so far purely a hypothetical figure.'

'My learned friend seems strangely sensitive about this point,' said Garfield. 'That an accomplice was used is obvious from the fact that the jewellery was not found in the house.'

Conroy looked from one of them to the other. 'No need to get heated, gentlemen,' he said. 'I find you in order, Mr. Garfield. You may proceed.'

'Thank you, my lord.' Maitland sat down with a distinctly mutinous look. 'You used the morning-room, I think,' Garfield added, turning back to the accused, 'because you did not want to stay any longer than necessary in the study with your victim.'

'I'm glad you give me credit for so much proper feeling,' said Malcolm bitterly.

'You didn't let me finish, Mr. Harte. I was about to suggest, not any lack of callousness, but fear of detection.'

For the first time, the prisoner was not ready with his reply. When the silence had lengthened a little Garfield returned to the attack. 'Let us get back, then, to this question of your holiday, to the conversation you had with Mr. George DeLisle – '

'I've already told you everything about that.'

'I'm afraid I cannot accept the reason you gave me.'

'Well, you'll have to. Because it's the only one – '
There was no doubt about it, as it had done when Maitland saw him in the prison, even more than it had done then, the question made him uneasy. (I should have pressed the matter myself, not let him come into court with an unbelievable story.)

'Come now, Mr. Harte.' As he sensed the witness's discomfort Garfield's tone grew silkier. 'Did the deceased tell you what his reasons were for taking the rather arbitrary step of asking you to change your honeymoon plans?'

'No, he didn't tell me why.'

'Those plans were important to you.'

'Of course they were.'

'But you are asking us to believe that he told you the arrangements might have to be changed without explaining why.'

'That's how it was.' Malcolm sounded breathless now. (He's lying, and he's not happy about it. And that's because – I warned him about this too – he's lying on oath.)

'You will admit there must have been some reason behind his request.'

'I suppose so. Yes, of course there must have been.'

'Some good reason.'

'I suppose so,' said the witness again. He sounded sulky, but he was very near breaking-point. Maitland realised it, and very likely Garfield realised it too.

'But in that event, surely Mr. Henry DeLisle would have been a party to the arrangement.' Counsel for the Prosecution paused, and then added in a tone like a whiplash, 'Do you not think so, Mr. Harte?' And Malcolm's hands, which had been grasping the rail in front of him, released their hold and spread suddenly in an extravagant gesture, as if he were relinquishing his last hope.

'You're right, of course,' he said. 'It wasn't that.'

If Garfield was pleased with his success, nothing about his demeanour showed it. 'Perhaps you will explain that remark a little more fully to the jury,' he requested coldly.

'Mr. George hadn't said anything to me about changing my holiday. I wanted to see him for . . . another reason.' (*Now* he has to tell us. I could raise an objection, and perhaps give him time to think, but it may be better to get it over with. The truth this time, because his conscience dictates it.)

Garfield was following up on his advantage. 'That reason being, do doubt, the one I have suggested to you.'

'No!' But that was the last flash of spirit, his voice was dead as he continued. 'I was in debt. Well, I suppose I still am, because the money hasn't been repaid. It was quite a large sum, and Mr. Wyatt was pressing for repayment.'

'How large a sum?'

'Four hundred pounds.'

'How did you come to be in debt to that amount?'

'It happened gradually. We were going to places we couldn't afford . . . dinners . . . the opera . . . ballet. Not always the cheap seats, because Eleanor and Laurence . . . oh, well! I should have called a halt, but I didn't.'

'And you had no savings?'

'Only enough to take us on our honeymoon trip. Mr. George held those for me, otherwise the money would have been spent. I wanted to ask him to lend me the four hundred, and if not to release my holiday money straight away. I could at least have paid what I owed, even if it did mean telling Mary we couldn't go away as planned.'

Garfield let the silence lengthen a moment after that. Then he said in a tone that seemed to Maitland insufferably self-satisfied, 'At least, Mr. Harte, you will no longer deny that you had a motive, a very strong motive, for needing money.'

That wasn't the end of the prosecution's questions, of course, though effectively it might have been. Nor could Maitland let his client go without further examination, some attempt to retrieve a position that he felt was hopeless. But when he sat down at last, and the judge decided it was time to call a halt for the day, it was with the feeling that the battle was already lost.

MONDAY, the third day (continued)

The study door was open when he let himself into the house in Kempenfeldt Square, and as if the hint wasn't obvious enough Gibbs was hovering at the back of the hall. 'Sir Nicholas would like a word with you, Mr. Maitland.' Antony sighed, but the request was quite a reasonable one, it wasn't late. He went in to join his uncle.

What Sir Nicholas wanted was a full account of the day's events. He grimaced over the tale of Malcolm Harte's cross-examination, but made no comment; only when his nephew had finished did he ask, 'When you came to re-examine – ?'

'He admitted it was William Wyatt to whom he owed the money.'

'I should have thought – '

'You're quite right, of course, he didn't know it was Wyatt he was borrowing from, just some loan company with a fancy name that I can't remember offhand. The trouble wasn't to get him to talk at this stage, it was to stop him. He told the court before I could do anything about it that Wyatt had taken over the matter personally because he wanted to persuade Harte not to see so much of Eleanor in the future.'

'That was probably why the loan was made in the first place,' said Sir Nicholas thoughtfully. 'To give Wyatt a lever. A young man who can offer no security is hardly a good risk.'

'I expect you're right. Anyway, the more he said, the worse it got. The court was certainly left with the impression that he was desperate for money.'

'And then?'

'I asked him what Mr. George DeLisle's reaction to his request had been.'

'You were taking a chance.'

'At that stage, nothing could have made matters worse. I asked him and he said George had been nice about it, agreed to lend him what he needed. I think he was telling the truth, I think he was so appalled at finding himself lying under oath that the truth was shocked out of him. But at the same time I can't help having a sneaking feeling that perhaps he was acting under Wyatt's instructions to steal the jewellery. It makes such a neat story.'

'I certainly think it is a possibility you must bear in mind. Tell me, Antony, what would you have done if Conroy had decided to continue?'

'I'd have had to ask for an adjournment to call further witnesses. Geoffrey didn't really have time – '

'But, if I understand you, you have no reason to call these other witnesses unless you hear something from William Webster.'

'I shall know tonight if he has anything for me, I'm going to call him.'

'And if he has nothing to report?'

'I shall close my case without further witnesses.'

'And what do you think the court would have made of that manoeuvre?'

'Uncle Nick, it hasn't happened. Conroy adjourned without my having to say anything at all.'

'There is another thing that occurs to me. Supposing Webster's report is not what you wish to hear?'

'I explained the position fully to Harte. He told me to go ahead.'

'It could make for a difficult situation.'

'You don't need to tell me that.' He got up restlessly. 'I know what you're thinking, Uncle Nick. All these witnesses up my sleeve, and what the hell am I going to ask them?'

'I cannot help hoping' – Sir Nicholas was seriously worried, or he would not have been speaking so quietly – 'that you will, after all, find no occasion to call any one of them.'

'Who lives may learn. I can't tell you the answer to that until I've talked to Father William.'

'No, I suppose not. You'd better get along, Antony. Jenny will be wondering what has happened to you. But remember, I want to be kept informed.'

'I shan't forget.'

And, because he wasn't expecting it, Jenny had news for him when he got upstairs. She came out into the hall as soon as she heard the door. 'Father William telephoned, Antony. He wants to see you.'

His first reaction was one of sheer surprise, then came the thought that it couldn't possibly be good news, not on the kind of day it had been. 'I suppose I'd better go and see him right away,' he suggested, rather half-heartedly.

'No, he said he'd be busy until after ten o'clock. And he wants to see you, a phone call won't do. That should mean something important, shouldn't it?'

'We'll hope for the best. Get me a drink, love. I've had one hell of a day.'

He was on his second sherry, and beginning to feel almost human again, when the phone rang. Jenny answered it, but turned with the receiver in her hand a moment later. 'It's Inspector Sykes.'

'Chief Inspector,' Antony corrected her automatically as he crossed the room to take her place. 'Should you be phoning me?' he asked when the first greetings – Sykes being particular about such things – had been exchanged.

'I think in the circumstances, Mr. Maitland, there can be no harm.' Sykes's voice was as placid, as comfortably north-country, as ever. 'I have something to communicate to you, but it has no ostensible connection with the case now before the court.'

'I see.'

The detective gave his deep chuckle. 'I don't suppose you do, Mr. Maitland, but one good turn deserves another, and its's something you may like to know. Lady Bowling is dead.'

There was a moment of dead silence before Antony said, foolishly, 'How do you mean . . . dead?'

'Murdered,' said Sykes. There was some amusement in his voice, not altogether suitable to the subject. 'I thought you'd find that interesting.'

'Well, I know I should be exclaiming in horror, and I'm sorry, of course. But . . . in heaven's name, Sykes, why?'

'That I can't tell you.'

'At least you can tell me how. What happened?'

'She was found this morning, very early, in Shelley Place, one of those narrow streets not far from Covent

Garden. To all appearances she'd been pushed out of a car.'

'That doesn't – '

'I'm getting to that, all in good time,' said Sykes, declining to be hurried. 'She was strangled with a silk scarf her husband says she was wearing when she left the house on Sunday evening. It was still round her neck.'

'Are you baffled, or have you a very good idea – ?'

'It's not my case, Mr. Maitland, I don't feel I can go into any more detail.'

'Well, I'm grateful to you, Chief Inspector. I am, indeed.'

'I ought to warn you, Mr. Maitland, I don't think you've a hope of using this as a red herring in court. Unless you could show some connection – '

'Don't worry, my mind isn't running on those lines. You have given me an idea though.'

'What sort of an idea?' The amusement had turned to suspicion now. 'If you know something we don't, Mr. Maitland – '

'I haven't a clue. And that, oddly enough, is the exact truth. No, Chief Inspector, this is something I have to work out for myself. You'll hear about it soon enough, if I do.'

'Then I suppose I must be content with that. Knowing you, I shouldn't have expected anything else. Well, if there's nothing else, I'll say good night, Mr. Maitland.'

'Good night to you, and I'm grateful, really I am.'

'That's what I'm afraid of,' said Sykes obscurely; and rang off.

There was a delay then while he put Jenny in the picture, but the time was well spent, it served to clear his mind. 'I'll have to see Sir Leonard Bowling,' he said regretfully, getting up, and then stooping to pick up his glass and drain it.

'But, Antony, not this evening!'

'It can't be helped, I . . . you don't think I'm looking forward to it, do you, love?'

'Of course not. But – '

'Don't fuss, Jenny. I'll be tact itself.' So far as I can, he added to himself, and in all the circumstances that may not be very far. 'Can you keep dinner warm for me?' he added, by way of a diversion.

'It's only a casserole. I'll turn the oven low.'

He would have liked to walk, to give himself the opportunity for reflection, but time was beginning to press on him. Better go round into Avery Street and pick up a cab, and trust to the inspiration of the moment when he came face to face with Sir Leonard.

This time he had given no notice of his coming, and wasn't surprised to be greeted with the information that 'Sir Leonard is not receiving visitors.' It took him only a moment to locate a card, to print on the back – because nobody could ever read his handwriting – A MATTER OF THE UTMOST IMPORTANCE.

'Give that to Sir Leonard,' he said. 'He may change his mind.' And sure enough, after a few minutes the man came back and stood aside to let him enter. Only as he turned from closing the door a spark of humanity showed for the first time.

'You know he's under a great strain today, don't you, sir?'

'I do,' Antony told him soberly. Indeed, he had been thinking of little else since Sykes had told him . . .

Bowling, as might have been expected from their last encounter, received him coldly. 'You say,' – he made a show of consulting the card, but it was clear he didn't need to – 'a matter of the utmost importance. I imagine that must be true, for you to intrude upon me at a time like this.'

'It's quite true. I've only just heard the news, and I'm sorry, deeply sorry – '

'I am quite willing to take your regrets as read, Mr. Maitland.' (Now, how was he going to get through to the chap in this mood? He's only seeing me at all because, in spite of everything, he's curious.) 'Please come to the point without delay.'

'It isn't all that easy,' said Antony truthfully. 'You weren't in court today, of course – '

'Naturally not.'

' – but if you had been you would have heard Malcolm Harte give evidence. I think you are perceptive enough to have realised, as I did because I am beginning to know him well by this time, that he threw away his last chance of an acquittal for a scruple.'

'That is interesting, of course, but I fail to see – '

'He admitted under cross-examination that he was in debt, to the tune of four hundred pounds, and that was why he wanted to talk to George DeLisle.'

'You mean, I suppose, that this comparatively small sum of money – '

'Comparatively small, Sir Leonard. An awful lot if you haven't got it.'

Bowling inclined his head, in acknowledgement, Antony thought, of the truth of this remark. 'You are implying, I think, that the motive for the crime is now even more strongly apparent.'

'Yes, but you see, I don't think he did either the theft or the murder.'

'Still, that is hardly my concern.'

'I should have thought you'd have been interested in justice.'

'In principle, of course, but . . . Mr. Maitland, you must see that today of all days – '

'I'm not talking about abstract justice. I'm talking about who killed your wife.'

'I . . . but . . . there can be no connection.'

'Do you like coincidences?'

'They do occur.'

'Not on this scale. I think the same person who killed George DeLisle is responsible – '

'But why? In heaven's name, why?'

'Because she knew too much.' Bowling did not attempt to answer that, and after a moment's pause he went on, 'If you're not interested in being the instrument of bringing the murderer to justice, you might at least spare a thought for the man who is wrongfully accused.' (I'm banking heavily on the fact that he's essentially a fair-minded man. If not, he'll probably throw me out within the next two minutes.) 'It would make a good story for the *Courier*, for instance. They rather go in for campaigns against injustice.'

'At the moment I am hardly interested – '

'No, of course. I'm just trying to get my point over. There's this chap, five months in prison already and the prospect of a life sentence. If he's innocent, and I think he is, that's everybody's concern.'

There was a silence after that, while several seconds ticked away. 'You're right, of course,' said Bowling at last. 'But I don't see what I can do about it.'

'You can tell me now, and repeat in court tomorrow, what you heard when you went into the hall a little before eleven o'clock on the night of the murder.'

This time the silence lengthened appreciably before Sir Leonard spoke. 'I wonder if you know what you're asking of me,' he said then in a reflective tone.

'I know very well. I'm sorry, but if you were in my place – '

'Yes, I appreciate your position. Very well, Mr. Maitland, I'll do what you want. But it won't be easy, you know.'

Antony was fumbling in his pocket for an envelope

156

on which to make notes. He thought, 'Nothing worth while ever is,' but the words were too trite, he did not repeat them aloud.

Jenny declared that the casserole was overcooked, but he enjoyed it anyway, though perhaps only, as she also said, dolefully, because by that time he was so hungry. 'And I know you think you know what Father William is going to tell you,' she added, as he took his coffee cup to a chair by the fire, 'but what if it's something quite different?'

'Then I shall have to think again.'

'But after that *awful* interview with Sir Leonard.' He had told her about it while they ate. 'It doesn't bear thinking of. And, Antony, even if things do turn out as you expect, it's going to be fantastically difficult.'

'Yes, love, I know. But I have to try everything, you do see that?'

'Of course. It's only . . . what Uncle Nick said . . . if you don't pull it off.'

'If I don't pull it off Garfield will have some amusement at my expense during his closing speech. I shan't die of it, love. In any case, I can't let that stop me. Think of Malcolm Harte.'

'I am thinking of him,' said Jenny, sighing. 'I suppose you really are convinced now that's he innocent.'

'Funnily enough, I am, in spite of his admission today in court. Besides, I think I know what really happened. I explained that.'

'The thing is, you've got no proof.'

'You don't have to remind me,' he said rather wearily. 'It's getting late, Jenny, I'd better be going, or Father William will have gone to bed.'

But William Webster was waiting for him; in the shop itself, not the living-quarters behind, from the speed with which he answered the bell. There was the grille to unlock, and close again carefully, and then they were making their way through the dimness of the shop towards the lighted doorway at the back that led to Father William's own domain.

As before, the visitor was guided towards the one arm-chair. Father William perched himself on the hard one he seemed to prefer, and beamed on his companion. 'I have what you want, Mr. Maitland. I admit, I don't see how it's going to help you, but I have what you want.'

'I wonder,' said Antony, thinking of his conversation with Jenny, and shifting his position a little because his shoulder was troubling him, 'whether it is actually what I should like to hear.'

'You have your own ideas about this matter,' said the old man shrewdly. 'Well, I shouldn't be surprised by that.'

'Tell me first, did Malcolm Harte steal the jewellery?'

'No.'

'Well, thank goodness for that anyway.'

'I've been following the case in the newspapers, Mr. Maitland. There was no premeditation, as the prosecution assumes. The man who stole the jewellery sold it himself to a buyer, with no go-between. But he did have an accomplice, whom he let into the house, and who was to have opened the safe for him.'

'So it was just George DeLisle's bad luck that he was still in the study – '

'Exactly.'

'That argues that the robbery was planned to take place after everyone had retired for the night. That makes sense,' said Antony thoughtfully.

'It would be interesting to know whether your deduction as to the guilty party corresponds with my knowledge.'

'If the man was a member of the party that night – '

'He was.'

' – it wasn't really a very difficult problem, or so I thought. But I had two props on which I based my argument, and one of them you've kicked out from under me.'

'Your argument may still be valid, for all that.'

'Let's see. What I thought was that the criminal must have been one of the two men not actually staying in the house, because the murder and the theft were discovered so soon that no one else would have had time to leave, hide the jewellery, and return. But if there was an accomplice – '

Father William had been nodding his head in a magisterial manner, but now he put up a hand to interrupt. 'He was to open the safe. He wasn't a person whom anyone at all knowledgeable would trust out of his sight with a valuable haul.'

'I see. Then the argument may still stand. *If* it does . . . of those two men, one can be assumed to have some acquaintance with the criminal fraternity from the nature of his employment. Laurence Blake is a crime reporter for the *Courier*.'

'I have the feeling that there is more to it than that. That you don't base your opinion only on those two facts.'

'There is more. Much more. I think I know how he returned to the house, and why he committed the crime. But you haven't told me . . . am I right?'

'Do I need to confirm it?' asked Father William, amused. 'You seem very sure of your facts.'

'I'd be surer still if you'd tell me – '

'Oh, yes, you're quite right. He sold the jewellery to a buyer of my acquaintance, whose name I need not trouble you with. I'm afraid there would be very little hope of identifying any of the jewellery now, most of the pieces will have been broken up already.'

'I suppose so.'

'You don't seem very pleased that I can confirm your deductions.'

Antony was thinking of the battle he was in for, next day in court. He wasn't really very hopeful of the outcome. 'Look here, Father William,' he demanded, 'do you know any of this of your own knowledge?'

'I'm afraid not.' William Webster was regretful. 'And my informant – though he would not lie to me – would not make a good witness, even if he could be persuaded into court.'

'The accomplice – '

'I was not told his name, only that he existed. Mind you, it would not be difficult, I imagine, for the police to find him, once they knew his principal's name.'

'If they'd look. Can you imagine the reception I'd get, going to them with a tale like this, Father William? No proof.'

'They are not, by definition, the most credulous of men,' Father William agreed sadly.

'Never mind.' Antony spoke more briskly. 'I'm grateful to you anyway,' he added, getting up.

'Now that our business is concluded, will you not share a nightcap with me?' the old man asked, obviously prepared to make a night of it.

'I'd like to, but better not. There's work to be done before morning.' But he was not thinking of that as he made his way home, on foot this time, but of Malcolm Harte, and how little chance there really was of getting a verdict in his favour.

Sir Nicholas had kidnapped Jenny, as was his custom when his curiosity was aroused, and they were both waiting for him in the study when Antony went in. The older man took one look at his nephew's face and stated flatly, 'You've got your proof that your client is innocent.'

Antony came across to the fireplace, moving rather stiffly, as he always did when he was more conscious than usual of the ache in his shoulder. 'Proof enough for me, Uncle Nick. Perhaps even for you. But nothing for the court.'

'Jenny has been explaining to me – ' He wasn't altogether to be blamed for the acerbity in his tone, Antony considered; Jenny's explanations were notoriously complicated. 'I think I have got a fair idea of the strategy you intend to use, but how you can be foolish enough to think you can do anything on direct examination I fail to see.'

'Sir Leonard has agreed to co-operate.' He sounded almost as tired as he felt, and Jenny gave him an anxious look. He caught the glance, and shook his head at her slightly. Might as well let Uncle Nick have his way.

'In the circumstances, I call that uncommonly decent of him.'

'So do I.'

'Some day you must explain to me how you had the gall – '

'I thought there was something he was concealing, and once I realised what it probably was – '

'You thought . . . you *guessed*!' said Sir Nicholas tartly. The word was anathema to him. 'But what is more important at the moment, what do you expect to happen tomorrow in court?'

'I shall call Bowling, and Wyatt, and Blake, in that order.'

'What the devil can Wyatt tell you?'

'He lied about the time he left the drawing-room. I think he saw or heard something too, and knowing what we do about his undercover activities he may have had good reason for suppressing his knowledge.'

'But you have no idea what?'

'Now that I am assured of Harte's innocence, it can't be anything damaging, at least.'

'I envy you your light-heartedness,' said Sir Nicholas bitterly. Antony smiled for the first time since he had come in.

'I wouldn't exactly say I felt light-hearted about it, Uncle Nick. But I can't let the matter go to the jury without at least trying – '

'And what will Garfield be doing while you are "trying"?' asked his uncle.

'Adding a few choice phrases to his closing speech, I should think. It's no good, Uncle Nick,' he added, as Sir Nicholas opened his mouth to speak again. 'You were my mentor . . . remember? You told me never to leave a stone unturned.'

'I am quite sure,' said Sir Nicholas, sitting up the better to emphasise his point, 'that, whatever I did or did not tell you, I never expressed myself at any time in so vile a cliché.' But the reminder had not been without its effect. Both Antony and Jenny accepted a nightcap at his insistence, but when they had drunk it he let them go without further argument.

TUESDAY, the fourth day

He went early to chambers next morning, to put Derek Stringer in the picture, and Geoffrey Horton was there too, by arrangement. Derek was silent when he had finished, though he looked thoughtful, as well he might; Geoffrey was frankly appalled. 'It's all very well if it comes off,' he said. '*If*. But I honestly don't think you've got a hope in hell.'

Antony, maddeningly, agreed with him quite meekly; but although the argument raged for as long a time as they had at their disposal, there was no turning him from what he intended to do. Geoffrey was still simmering gently, and Derek was still thoughtful, when they arrived at the court.

There was a small stir among the spectators when Sir Leonard Bowling's name was called. Some of them at least had evidently read of his bereavement. Maitland, watching the jury for some similar sign of interest, couldn't decide which of them, if any, had heard the news. They were self-conscious, aware of being in the public eye, and not one of them was going to betray his feelings by so much as the flicker of an eye-lash.

Bowling was calm enough as they went through the preliminaries, but Maitland was only too well aware of the strain his witness was under. 'You agreed voluntarily to give evidence at this trial, did you not, Sir Leonard?' he asked.

'I did.'

'In spite of the tragic death of Lady Bowling, of which you learned only yesterday?'

'My lord!'

'I think perhaps the death of a witness may be regarded as relevant, Mr. Garfield. What do you think, Mr. Maitland?'

'I am trying very hard not to be controversial, my lord,' said Maitland in an injured tone. 'I introduced the fact of Lady Bowling's death, not to argue its relevance, but to give the court some idea of Sir Leonard's strong sense of duty in coming here at such a time.'

'Very well. Will that satisfy you, Mr. Garfield?'

'It must be as your lordship pleases,' said Garfield non-committally, and seated himself again.

'You may proceed, Mr. Maitland,' said Conroy. He

was amiability itself this morning, and Antony wondered uneasily how long it would last.

But first there was an account of Saturday, the thirteenth June, to be got through . . .

If that was all the witness's evidence amounted to, they might as well have left the poor man to brood over his tragedy in peace. Funny Maitland hadn't said the woman had been murdered, made you think, a thing like that; coincidence, perhaps, but all the same . . .

The ninth juror was a man, whom Maitland had noticed particularly owing to his strong resemblance to a fox terrier. It was the first time the slightest doubt of the accused man's guilt had occurred to him, and even now he didn't give it very much consideration. The evidence was clear, and there were Harte's admissions too. It wasn't even as if he could feel very much sympathy for him. A chap like that, steady job and all, getting into debt.

Wonder how much he was paid. Henry DeLisle had given the impression of a sharp man, probably not over-generous. Still, it was probably more than he, the juror, was getting as a postman, and he'd like the chance, nice soft job, indoors in the bad weather, not wearing out shoe leather making deliveries.

So if he got into debt in spite of all his advantages, that was very much his own fault. Funny to think that if George DeLisle had agreed to making him a loan none of this would have happened. Most likely not. But you could see the temptation, being turned down – as he must have been – seeing the jewellery so conveniently at hand, and the lump of amethyst . . . and probably too Harte had thought at that moment of the difference between the DeLisles' fortunes and his own. Only natural that he should have done so. Said himself he felt out of place at that posh weekend, every one of the guests with money except him.

The chap next to him now, chap on his left, he was a lucky one. Perfectly tailored suit, gold wristwatch, gold signet ring, gold cuff-links. He'd like half the chance to be turned out like that. Of course, he'd done his best, but his suit sagged in the wrong places, his watch lost five minutes a day (at least, it was regular about that), he didn't wear a ring and his cuff-links came from Woolies. Not good for a working chap like him to be here among all the toffs. Made you realise how unlucky you'd always been. But Maitland . . . there was an alertness about him now, as though he was coming to some special point. Something new, perhaps . . .

' . . . so, Sir Leonard, you agree that you left the drawing-room that evening, during the hour that you spent there in conversation with Mr. Henry DeLisle and Mr. Wyatt, and you would not be surprised if I told you that it was three minutes to eleven when you returned.'

'I am a little vague about it, but that fits in well enough with my own recollection.'

'You are quite clear, however, about the time Mr. William Wyatt left the drawing-room.'

'Not to the minute, no. But certainly after I did, only a few minutes before we went upstairs ourselves.'

'Thank you. You are also clear, I believe, about your own actions while you were out of the room.'

'Yes.'

'What did you do, Sir Leonard?' asked Maitland encouragingly, when the witness fell silent.

'I went to the morning-room and listened.'

'I must ask you to explain to us, Sir Leonard, what made you take this course of action?'

'Yes.' Again there was a silence, but this time Maitland did not attempt to break it. 'I had been aware for some time that my wife had a lover,' said Bowling at last, his voice quiet but perfectly clear in the stillness of the courtroom, 'and that evening I learned for the first time definitely who it was.'

'How did that come about?'

'I overheard a snatch of conversation, when we were gathered in the drawing-room before dinner. They were standing a little aloof from the others, and could not have expected that anyone could hear what was said. But I have very acute hearing, and besides, I was on the alert.'

'What exactly did you hear?'

'My lord!'

'Yes, Mr. Garfield, but we cannot recall Lady Bowling to give her evidence on this point. I think we may hear at least what she had to say,' said Mr. Justice Conroy patiently.

'Did you understand that, Sir Leonard? You may tell us only what you overheard your wife saying,' said Maitland. (That ought to be enough.)

'It was only a few words here and there. I heard her say, "As soon as I can get away", and, "The room behind this one". And, quite clearly, "I'll open the window for you". In any case, the man's voice did not carry so well.'

'You took it they were arranging an assignation?'

'Yes.'

'So you think Lady Bowling was going down to the morning-room by appointment, when she saw my client on the stairs?'

'It is the only conclusion I can come to. I should explain that Mrs. DeLisle showed my wife round the house soon after we arrived, so she was familiar with the lay-out.'

Maitland turned a little. 'The "room behind this one", my lord, is the morning-room. If you will look at the plan – ' He waited until he saw the judge's head bent obediently over the architect's drawing, until each member of the jury was similarly occupied, and then looked back at Sir Leonard Bowling again. 'You had, I think, something more to tell us about this knowledge

'. . . this fear . . . you had concerning Lady Bowling.'

'Yes, I – ' It was obvious that, to him, this was the most difficult part of his disclosures. ' – I was afraid, I was almost sure that she meant to leave me. Buying the jewellery was – was an attempt at bribery, I suppose.'

'An attempt to persuade her not, after all, to take such a drastic step?'

'Something like that.' The re-wording of his admission seemed to give him back a little confidence.

'Tell me – I appreciate that in the circumstances this is a difficult question, Sir Leonard – '

'If my learned friend is so concerned with his witness's feelings,' snapped Garfield suddenly, 'why does he continue to harrow them with these quite irrelevant questions?'

The judge looked from Counsel for the Prosecution to Counsel for the Defence, and then back at Garfield again. 'I am inclined to allow the defence a good deal of latitude,' he said.

'Yes, my lord, that is very proper, of course. But in a matter that can have no bearing – '

'Has it a bearing, Mr. Maitland?'

'My lord, I can only say that if you will allow me to continue – '

Conroy did not wait for him to finish. 'Very well, Mr. Maitland,' he said, still with that suspicious affability; but the sting was in the tail of that remark. 'You may continue, for the time being.'

'I am obliged to your lordship. I was about to ask you, Sir Leonard, whether you think that Lady Bowling in, let us say, a second marriage, would have been content with a standard of living lower than the one she knew with you.'

'I believe' – again he was fumbling for words – 'I believe that during the last few months it has only been material considerations that kept her with me.'

'I see. But in spite of your fears, in spite of the fact that you had not purchased the jewellery you had promised her, she did stay with you.'

'Yes.' He paused, looking round the court, and then back at Maitland again. 'There is something else that I should tell you. During the last two days of her life, from the time she gave evidence in this court to the time she left the house on Sunday evening, she seemed nervous, almost distraught, quite unlike herself.'

'You say Lady Bowling left the house on Sunday evening. Did you in fact see her again?'

'No. I thought – God forgive me! – when she didn't return I thought she had gone to her lover.'

Garfield had been a little slow off the mark. He got up now with a face like a thundercloud. 'My lord, you said you were willing to allow my friend a good deal of latitude, but do you not think he is abusing your consideration?'

'Indeed I do, Mr. Garfield.' His lordship, though calmer than counsel, looked almost equally put out. 'Mr. Maitland, if you cannot conduct your examination with more propriety, with more consideration for the relevance of the matter introduced – '

'I am extremely sorry, my lord,' said Maitland, not succeeding altogether in hiding from the judge the fact that things, for the moment, were going just as he wished. 'My remaining questions will be extremely to the point, I promise you.'

'Very well, Mr. Maitland, very well.'

As an invitation to proceed it lacked something in warmth, but counsel chose to ignore that. 'I am obliged to your lordship,' he said, and turned to the witness again. 'So now we come back, Sir Leonard, to your actions when you left the drawing-room that evening. You say you went down the hall to the door of the morning-room and listened. What did you hear?'

'My wife's voice, and the man's. I couldn't tell what they were saying, but they sounded to be arguing.'

'But you are certain it was Lady Bowling?'

'Quite certain. I could distinguish her tones quite clearly.'

'And the man?'

'It was, as I had expected, the one I heard her talking to earlier in the evening. I knew his voice quite well too, and there could be no mistaking it.'

'And the man's name?'

'Laurence Blake.'

Even the jury looked interested at that; it caused another stir among the spectators, another cry of 'Silence!' Maitland stood a moment longer, looking round the court as though assessing the effectiveness of what had been said. Then he said, 'That is all, thank you, Sir Leonard,' and sat down. But that was the easy part of his day's work, the hard part was still to come.

Garfield got up, and for the first time in Maitland's knowledge of him – probably for the first time in his life – he seemed unsure of himself. After a moment the judge prompted gently, 'Yes, Mr. Garfield?'

'My lord, I am at a loss how to proceed in a matter which has so little relevance to the case being tried.'

'I allowed the evidence, Mr. Garfield. You must make of it what you can.'

'As your lordship pleases.' Maitland, glancing round, caught his eye, and couldn't resist a sympathetic grin; which, being interpreted correctly by his opponent, added nothing to his pleasure in the situation. 'You say, Sir Leonard, that you had been aware for some time that Lady Bowling had a lover.' Garfield had regained his confident, almost disdainful air, but Maitland was perfectly well aware that he was plunging wildly. 'You did not tell us, however, how you knew this.'

'A hundred and one little things. Unexplained absences . . . a silence . . . a withdrawal.'

'Intangibles,' said Garfield scornfully.

'They added up to certainty. And I may say that I had suspected that the man was Laurence Blake before that day. That was why I did my best to overhear their conversation.'

At that Garfield was guilty of a most uncharacteristic piece of theatricality. Turning to the jury he shrugged his shoulders, abandoning a witness in whose evidence he had no conceivable interest. 'I have no further questions, Sir Leonard,' he said.

The tenth juror, as his neighbour had noticed, was something of a dandy. What his fellow-juror hadn't realised, however, was that the perfectly tailored suit was off-the-peg (though worn with an air), the gold cuff-links weren't gold at all, and the signet ring had been a gift from his godmother – who hadn't remembered him in her will – on his twenty-first birthday. In other respects, his way of life might be enviable. He lived modestly, without a regular job, on a legacy from his parents, the income from which he occasionally augmented by a lucky evening at the bridge table.

Now, as Sir Leonard Bowling stepped down and the next witness was called, he was reviewing the course of the trial in the light of the new evidence. Difficult to see what the defence was driving at. Of course, the open window in the morning-room had been a point in the prosecution's case, and now it seemed it had been opened by that smashing looking piece of goods, Sarah Bowling, to readmit her lover to the house. Maitland had introduced very neatly the fact that she was dead and couldn't be recalled to give evidence on that point, and there was a coincidence if you liked! Or was it a coincidence? If Harte hadn't killed his employer after all . . .

But that was nonsense. There were the fingerprints to account for; the fact that he admitted lying to the police and even, ap-

parently, to his own counsel; and the further uncomfortable fact of his indebtedness. And the prosecution could say – would say, no doubt, when Garfield's turn came to address the jury – that the study window had been used to hand the jewellery to the mysterious accomplice whom the police had not been able to produce. Was there something a bit thin about that, after all? Not really; it would be so much more convenient, with George DeLisle safely dead, than crossing the hall to the morning-room. But it would be interesting to hear what his companions in the jury-box had to say about that.

He glanced at his watch – the gold watch his neighbour had noticed, it really was gold, and a Bulova Accutron as well – and thought a little complacently that it had been a bit of luck, finding it in the street like that. A new strap needed, certainly, even so it was difficult to see how the original owner hadn't noticed its loss. But no damage from the fall it must have had to the hard pavement. That just showed you that quality counts.

Debby had been impressed, though rather inclined to think the money might have been spent on her. But he had told her he'd won it at the Club, staked his own tuppenny ha'penny affair against it with an opponent who was half drunk. Even at that she'd been a little shocked, said it was taking an unfair advantage; if he'd told her the truth ten to one she'd have made him go to the police. And only too likely it would have been claimed within the time limit, a valuable piece like that.

What it told him now when he consulted it was that there seemed to be some delay in locating the witness, William Wyatt, whose name had been called. And then, just as the judge opened his mouth, probably to chide the defence counsel for his witness's tardiness, the man appeared. And the first thing you noticed about him was that he looked flustered . . .

Maitland noticed it too, and glanced round at Horton with just a hint of triumph in his look. Of course, Wyatt had been surprised to receive a subpoena, his evidence as given to the two of them on Saturday morning could hardly be considered earth-shaking, but he hadn't dared hope that the summons would upset the self-styled financier so much. Now, if old Conroy didn't come down on him too hard . . .

He asked the routine questions, a boring preliminary to be got through as quickly as possible. Now that it came to the point, Wyatt's manner was an odd mixture of the anxiety that had been so evident and a touch of aggressiveness, as though he were daring counsel to demonstrate why he had been dragged here out of his ordinary routine. Yes, he had been a guest at the De-Lisles' the weekend in question, had stayed the night with them, not that anybody got much sleep. He and his wife had arrived at about six-thirty; the DeLisles were old friends, 'And, of course,' he went on, 'we knew the Bowlings quite well too. They were already there when we arrived, and young Harte and the girl from the office, Mary Reynolds.'

'Both of whom were previously known to you?'

'Miss Reynolds is an old school friend of my daughter, Eleanor. I have known her for some time.'

'You had had some dealings with my client, Mr. Harte, however.'

'I was acquainted with him.'

'Also through his friendship with your daughter?'

'I had seen him at the shop.'

'I see. That wasn't quite what I meant, however. If you have any scruples about giving evidence incriminating to my client, Mr. Wyatt, I must tell you that he has admitted to us that he was in debt to you to the tune of four hundred pounds.'

The witness had a blank look for that, and then said rather hesitantly, 'That makes a difference, of course. Yes, there was that one transaction. Not that I was concerned in it directly, but when the matter was referred to me I felt I should help him in view of the fact that Eleanor regarded him as a friend.'

'That is very understandable.' Maitland's tone was smooth as silk. 'But it was also in view of his friendship with your daughter – was it not? – that you later pressed him for payment.'

'I did not like the association,' said Wyatt defiantly.

(Perhaps I've shaken him. Well, there's only one way of finding out. If I can succeed in sounding thoroughly sinister . . .) 'But money-lending is not your only activity, is it?' (Heaven send that he interprets that as I want him to, not as the jury will, merely as a reference to his reputable dealings in the financial world.)

'One transaction can hardly be considered to qualify me for membership of that profession,' said Wyatt rallying. But for all that he was visibly shaken. Maitland smiled at him.

'I do not wish to – to press the matter,' he said. 'Shall we go back to the night of the thirteenth June? I am interested in the latter part of the evening, after the two dinner guests had gone, and the ladies and Malcolm Harte had retired to bed.'

'Well . . . we were left chatting together in the drawing-room, Henry DeLisle, Leonard Bowling, and I.'

'So we have been given to understand. Now, it seems that during the hour you were together both you and Sir Leonard had occasion to leave the drawing-room.'

'That is true. I happened to look at my watch at three minutes to eleven, and that was just after Leonard – Sir Leonard – came back.'

'I hope you can be as accurate about the time you were absent yourself, Mr. Wyatt.'

'I am a little vague about it, I admit.'

'Have a bash at it,' urged counsel, forgetting himself.

'Then, I think it was immediately before Sir Leonard

went out, probably between a quarter and ten to eleven.'

'I must tell you, Mr. Wyatt, that does not accord with Sir Leonard's recollection. According to evidence that has been given in this court – '

'I have said I am vague about it.'

'Would you agree with Sir Leonard's estimate then? He says it was certainly after his own absence, and no more than a few minutes before you all retired yourselves.'

'That was at eleven-thirty.' The witness was frowning over his reply, obviously uncertain as to where these questions were leading. 'If Sir Leonard remembers clearly it is more than I do. I can't argue with him.'

'Then we may take it that you agree you were absent from the drawing-room for several minutes at about twenty past – twenty-five past? – eleven.'

'Yes, that is correct.'

'What did you do during your absence, Mr. Wyatt?'

'Why, I – '

'I may say that I fully appreciate that your particular circumstances made you unwilling to give this information voluntarily to the police, bearing in mind that other occupation we spoke of. If you wish me to go into further details – '

Garfield was on his feet. The judge leaned forward and said in the gentle tone that spelled trouble, 'Mr. Maitland, are you not verging on the impropriety of cross-examining your own witness?'

'I am sorry, my lord.' Enough had been said anyway. If that veiled threat didn't do the trick, nothing would. 'May I repeat my question to the witness?'

'If you must, Mr. Maitland, if you must.' There was a note of petulance in the judge's tone. (He doesn't know what I'm driving at, but he's beginning to wonder . . .)

'I am obliged to your lordship. What did you do, Mr. Wyatt, during your absence from the drawing-room at about twenty past eleven on the evening of the thirteenth June last?'

Even then the answer didn't come straight away. Wyatt looked round the courtroom wildly, as though seeking some avenue of escape. Then he turned back to counsel, but evidently found no comfort in his expression. 'I went to the study,' he said, in a voice that was suddenly over-loud.

'Thank you, Mr. Wyatt.' If he was relieved, there was nothing to show it. 'And what did you find there?'

'Mr. George DeLisle was writing letters at the desk.' Even the jury, concerned as each one was with his own image, showed signs of animation at that. The spectators were frankly excited, and again there were calls for silence. Mr. Justice Conroy turned on counsel a look in which there was very little of loving kindness, but Maitland was absorbed in his witness and took no notice.

'What then, Mr. Wyatt?'

'We had a brief conversation together, and then I left.'

'He was still in good health at that time?'

'Yes, certainly.'

'Did you see the jewellery while you were there?'

'It was not in evidence, but the designs – Henry's designs – were on the desk, pushed back to make room for the notepaper George was using.'

'You are telling us then – I want to be very clear about this, Mr. Wyatt, so that there may be no misunderstanding – you are telling us that Mr. George DeLisle was alive and well at a little before eleven-thirty on the night he died.'

'Yes, that is true.'

At which point Maitland abandoned his witness to the wolves, and Garfield got up to cross-examine.

'He gave him a bad time,' said Derek Stringer, as the waiter brought their pre-luncheon drinks and departed.

'That was only to be expected.' Maitland seemed to regard his responsibility in the matter lightly. 'After all, he made a hash of explaining why he wanted to see George – '

'Yes, *why* do you think he went to the study?'

'I think the jewellery drew him as a magnet draws iron.'

'But – '

'I don't mean he meant to steal it, just that he hoped to see it again. And with regard to the "bad time" you referred to, the reason he gave for lying to the police – that he didn't want to be suspected – didn't sound well in the circumstances.'

'What I can't understand is why he caved in like that.'

'*The wicked flee where no man pursueth,*' said Antony, a little smugly. 'He was wondering how much I knew.'

'If he'd realised you were guessing – '

'I meant specifically about his "other occupation",' Antony explained. 'He didn't want to risk a charge of perjury, which might have had results even more unpleasant than Garfield's cross-examination, and he didn't want to risk my airing my supposed knowledge of his undercover activities. It's a good thing,' he added thoughtfully, 'that Father William was right about that.'

'I suppose,' said Derek, thinking it out, 'that was the real reason he didn't admit having been to the study when the police first questioned him. If they were as wise as your friend about his doings they'd have been bound to have suspected him.'

'That's all very well.' Geoffrey, who had been brooding over his drink, came to life suddenly. 'You took a chance and it came off, but if it hadn't – '

'Let's not think about that.'

'I think we should.'

'I can't see why.'

'Because I want you to leave it there, Antony. Close your case when we get back to the court and leave it at that.'

'I want to talk to Laurence Blake,' said Maitland stubbornly.

'You won't get away with it twice,' Geoffrey warned him.

'Get away with what?'

'Trying to extract admissions from an unwilling witness on direct examination, and with no real evidence to back up your guesses either. You haven't anything to blackmail Blake with, remember. Besides, the jury must acquit Harte.'

'There's no must about it. Don't you agree with me?' he appealed to Stringer. 'Garfield has the last word, you know. He'll say the jewellery was handed out of the study window, not the morning-room, and that Harte went back to the study when everyone else had retired, probably knowing the combination of the safe – after all, he laid foundation for that, even if he seemed to have changed his mind about it later – and thinking George had gone to bed too. Besides, juries love fingerprints and the motive – his indebtedness to Wyatt – is one they can all understand. Don't forget, Garfield had the chance of cross-examining Wyatt on the subject, and stressed the point that he was pressing for repayment.'

'All the same, I think you should rest your case now, and not risk making a fool of yourself over Blake.'

'It seems to be a chance I've got to take,' said Antony. His tone had been light throughout the argument, but now it was suddenly sober.

Derek looked from one to the other of them and laughed. 'You won't persuade him, Geoffrey,' he said. 'You may as well stop trying.' And, fortunately, the waiter arrived back with their soup just at that moment.

But Antony was absent-minded throughout the meal, and left them before the coffee was served, with no more explanation than that he wanted to talk to Garfield. That left Derek and Geoffrey staring at each other; it seemed to both of them an unreasonable desire.

The jury were brought back into court a little early after the luncheon recess. The eleventh juror, a tall woman, a little overweight, with wiry grey hair and an expression of placid amiability, was glad enough to get away from the chatter in the jury room, to have a chance of thinking things out for herself. It seemed there had to be some reassessing, at least half her colleagues were talking of an acquittal, and though she realised there might be some second thoughts after Counsel for the Prosecution had his say, she felt herself the time had come when all the evidence was in and they must make up their minds for themselves. Which wasn't so easy.

It would be so simple to say, 'Not guilty,' and so end the matter, but she wasn't one who took her responsibilities as lightly as that. If he were guilty . . . a nasty, brutal, messy business it had been, and surely the perpetrator shouldn't be allowed to go free. To murder again perhaps. It wasn't as if you could count on life bringing its own punishment, as far as she could see those who deserved least fared the best, while the well-deserving . . .

Look at the years she'd spent looking after Father, no life of her own, existing as she did almost continuously in the company of a demanding, querulous old man. 'Won't be long now, girl,' he'd say to her; he'd still call her that, she supposed at eighty-eight all lesser ages seemed the same to him. 'Won't be long now,' when she'd nearly given up hoping. After so long, she wouldn't know what to do with her freedom when she got it, that was the trouble.

But in the end it had been so easy, he'd just slipped away quietly. Nothing to do with the fact that she'd forgotten his medicine and he — never one to take it without an argument — hadn't reminded her. The doctor had warned her, 'It's the only thing that keeps him going,' he'd said it more than once, but surely even he couldn't have been certain that that in the end had caused the old man's death. Just a moment's carelessness, that's all it had been, and the more she thought about it herself, the more certain she became that Father's time had come anyway. Certainly there was nothing to blame herself for.

But here her thoughts were, running on again, when she had meant to think quite dispassionately about the trial. She was startled now to find that the barristers had taken their places, the accused had been brought back to the dock, the judge had made his entrance. And against all expectation, here was the defence calling another witness, when she had been quite sure the case was complete . . .

If Maitland was looking for the same signs of ner-. vousness in Laurence Blake as had characterised Wyatt's entrance, he was disappointed. Blake had a confident, almost jaunty look about him. Of course, he knew nothing yet of the evidence that had been given that morning, unless he had met Wyatt or Bowling during the recess, which wasn't likely. They'd neither of them be in the mood for casual conversation, and had probably gone straight home when the opportunity offered.

But now that it came to the point, now that Blake

was actually in the witness box answering his routine questions, he had begun to wonder whether Geoffrey hadn't been right, after all. He would have some final words to say himself, as well as Garfield, and could surely have persuaded the jury . . . Uncle Nick could have done it, but he didn't have too much confidence in his own powers of persuasion. In any event, it was too late to think of that now.

'First, Mr. Blake, I want you to tell us about the evening of the thirteenth June last. You had been invited to dinner by Mrs. Grace DeLisle?'

'Yes, that's right.'

'Had you known the DeLisles previously?'

'I had met George DeLisle on business. Not the others. I owed my invitation to the fact that I was – that I am engaged to be married to one of the other guests.'

'I see. But you knew the firm, DeLisle Brothers, by repute, no doubt?'

'Certainly.'

'So you accepted the invitation?'

'I did. Eleanor – Miss Wyatt – my fiancée had told me about the showing of the jewellery that was pro-posed, and besides having the pleasure of her company for the evening I thought it would be interesting to see it.'

'And was it interesting?'

'It was.'

'So you arrived at the DeLisles' house – ?'

'I aimed to be there at about a quarter or ten to eight. I didn't consult my watch, as it happens, to see how well I had succeeded.'

'The point is immaterial. But I should like to know, Mr. Blake, what was the subject of your conversation with Lady Bowling in the drawing-room before dinner?'

For a moment the witness's look of surprise was almost comical. He stared at counsel open-mouthed before he recovered himself sufficiently to say, 'At this distance of time I can't tell you. It must have been something quite trivial, I was not well acquainted with the lady.'

'You are telling us she was almost a stranger to you?'

'Not that, no. I had met her socially, and as my employer's wife I suppose I paid her more attention than I should have to another chance-met acquaintance.'

'Then you cannot remember – '

'No, I can't.' This was said sharply. The veneer of confidence was wearing thin, but it wasn't time to get him rattled yet.

'It is later in the evening that interests us, after all.' Maitland changed course smoothly. 'You inspected the jewellery, I believe, along with the other guests, from approximately ten o'clock to ten-thirty.'

'That would be about right.'

'After which – ?' There was a pause. 'I am asking you what happened after that?' Maitland amplified.

'George DeLisle put the jewellery back in its cases, packed them in an attaché case, and said he was going to the study to write letters.'

'Have you been reading about this case, Mr. Blake?'

'Yes, of course. Besides, the reporter who is covering it for my paper is a friend of mine.'

'Then you will know that no signs of this letter-writing were found in the study.'

'I had supposed that to be because he had been killed before he could carry out his intention.'

'That is one theory. Not one to which I subscribe.' The witness had no comment to make, and counsel went on after a moment's pause. 'Mr. George DeLisle took the jewellery to the study with him?'

'He certainly took it out of the room with him. I am not sufficiently familiar with the plan of the house – '

'You did not know which door led to the study?'

'I do now. My friend showed me a plan.'

'So now we come to your own actions, Mr. Blake.'

'It was turned ten-thirty. Thurlow, another of the dinner guests, said it was time he went home, and I agreed and left at the same time.' He was beginning to be impatient of the questions; perhaps – though he was hiding it well – as angry as he had been on Sunday afternoon. 'I went straight home, I can't prove it, but Thurlow could tell you I had to move my car before he could get his out of the drive.'

'And what did you do after you had driven out into the road?'

'I went straight home, of course.' There was no doubt about the anger now, that was said with something of a snap. Maitland smiled at him.

'Of course,' he said gently. And then, 'I have no further questions.'

As he sat down again Stringer gave him a startled look, and Horton, forgetting himself, grabbed painfully at his shoulder. 'Look here – ' he began in a furious undertone. Maitland disentangled himself, but did not attempt any other reply than a shake of the head, and the one word, 'Wait.' But he breathed a silent sigh of relief as he saw Garfield come to his feet.

'There are . . . just a few questions, Mr. Blake,' said Counsel for the Prosecution.

It wasn't difficult to read Blake's thoughts. He had been prepared for Maitland's questions, had probably expected them to be pressed home more hardly, but Garfield was an unknown quantity. He turned warily to face this new adversary. 'Would it surprise you to know, Mr. Blake,' Garfield went on without any change of tone, 'that according to the witnesses we have heard today almost everything you have told us is a pack of lies?'

If he expected an answer, he didn't get one immediately. Blake looked wildly from Garfield to Maitland and back again, very much as though he couldn't believe his ears. Then he turned a little to face the judge and said in a strangled voice, 'My lord!'

Mr. Justice Conroy looked back at him gravely, and then turned his attention to Counsel for the Prosecution. If he was thinking, 'This is some new trick of Maitland's' there was nothing in his voice or countenance to indicate this, nothing but a sort of bland courtesy. 'Mr. Garfield?' he said.

'My lord, in view of what has been said in this court, it seems only right to try to get at the truth of the matter. In any event, your lordship will agree that I have the right to cross-examine one of the witnesses for the defence.'

The judge took his time over that. He too glanced at Maitland, a glance that might have been considered too sharp for comfort. 'You may proceed, Mr. Garfield,' he said.

Horton sat back in his place again, suddenly at ease. Stringer said under his breath, 'How the devil did you persuade him?' But Maitland took no notice of either of them. He was watching Blake's face.

'I do not believe,' said Garfield into the silence, 'that you have forgotten my question, Mr. Blake.'

'No, but I was taken by surprise. There is nothing to say except that I have told the truth. I – '

'You can tell us how, and why, you re-entered the DeLisles' home that Saturday night.'

'But I didn't – '

'How, Mr. Blake, and why?'

'This is ridiculous.' But he didn't sound as if he found it in any way amusing. 'I went straight home.'

Garfield, who was never guilty of levity, became at this point even more serious. 'Perhaps you are thinking that, with Lady Bowling dead, there is no one left who can give evidence to that effect.' Blake said nothing, he was staring at counsel in a fascinated way, and breathing hard as though he had been running. 'Let me tell you then that you were overheard arranging to meet her, and again overheard when you were talking to her in the morning-room. "It sounded as though they were arguing" were the words the witness used.'

There was a silence. Finally Blake said, as though each word cost him an effort, 'Yes, I did go back, but we only talked together for ten minutes – a quarter of an hour. Then I went home.'

'Lady Bowling admitted you to the house through the morning-room window?'

'Yes.'

'And why did you wish for this clandestine meeting, Mr. Blake?'

'Because I was desperate! I wanted her to go away with me. She wouldn't agree.'

'In spite of your engagement to Miss Wyatt?'

'In spite of that. Eleanor is a nice girl, but – '

'Why wouldn't Lady Bowling agree to go away with you?'

'I suppose she didn't love me enough.' If that was an attempt at flippancy, it was a dismal failure.

'May I make a different suggestion to you?' Garfield leaned forward a little, very stiff, very cold, very accusing. (Very impressive, Maitland thought, and I wouldn't like to be in Blake's shoes. But Uncle Nick would do it better.) 'May it not have been financial considerations that dictated Lady Bowling's decision to stay with her husband?'

'No. I don't know. Well, I think it may have been.'

'It would be helpful if you could make up your mind on the point,' Garfield pointed out in his most disapproving tone. Blake made no reply, but he didn't look away. He seemed as fascinated by counsel now as a rabbit might be by a snake. 'If my surmise is correct,' Garfield went on, 'that would mean that you were in desperate need of money. I believe "desperate" was your own word, was it not?'

'I did want . . . if I'd had money she'd have come to me . . . but I didn't want it enough to murder for it!'

'Nobody has mentioned the word murder to you, Mr. Blake.'

'No, but . . . that's what you're getting at, isn't it? You're trying to say – '

'I am wondering why, if you left after fifteen minutes' conversation with Lady Bowling, she didn't close the window behind you.'

'Because she wasn't there. She was annoyed with me, because I had promised . . . you're right, we were arguing . . . she went away and left me there.'

'What then?'

'I told you. I went home.'

'Even though you were desperate?'

'Yes!'

'As you had not the opportunity of hearing the previous witness I must tell you that George DeLisle was still alive at eleven-twenty that night.'

'Well, I know that. I – '

'How did you know?' Another blank silence. 'How did you know that?' Garfield repeated.

'I didn't, of course. I thought you meant ten-thirty.'

'Did you indeed?' Nothing could have exceeded the scepticism in Garfield's tone. 'May I suggest to you, Mr. Blake, that you knew George DeLisle was still alive at that hour because you saw him subsequently, because you went across to the study after the rest of the party had retired – '

Laurence Blake did not allow him to finish. His breath was still coming in heavy gasps. 'If you know it all,' he spat out, 'why do you bother to ask me?'

'It wasn't a confession, or anything like one,' said the twelfth juror, looking round at his companions, 'but I can tell you now, I never thought Harte was guilty.' It only showed you, he thought, how right could triumph, which was comforting for one who prided himself on keeping on the right side of the law, the right side of the ten commandments, come to that.

'Well, I admit,' – the seventh juror had an uneasy look about him – 'I did think he'd done it.' (Have I been guilty in the past of making false judgments, of spreading slander where the charge was unfounded? After today I can never be quite sure again.)

'But after what the prosecution said . . . that chap Garfield in his closing address. He admitted that the whole premise on which his case was founded had been destroyed.' That was the foreman, in a tone which demanded their attention. 'To my mind there's no need for discussion. Harte was wrongly accused, and we're not asked to say about Blake. Does anyone disagree with that?'

'It's getting late,' said the sixth juror. (And why should that worry her? She wasn't in a hurry to get home.)

'That's true.' Now that it was over and she'd be back at her desk in the morning, the third juror had relaxed a little. 'All the same, we've got to be very sure – '

'Sure of what?' said the ninth juror belligerently.

'Of Harte's innocence, of course. But I am sure of that,' said the fourth juror happily. She'd have gone along, she supposed, if the majority had felt the other way, but this was much better.

'Wait a bit.' That was the ninth juror again. 'Blake didn't confess, Harte could have gone down to the study again. There are his fingerprints.'

'He explained those.'

'Yes, but do you suppose he or anybody else tells the whole truth when facing a murder charge?' The fifth juror sounded a little belligerent too.

'Perhaps not.' The foreman was placatory. 'But nobody can tell me that fellow Blake didn't have something on his conscience.' There was a chorus of agreement. 'In the circumstances it would be obviously impossible – the judge came as near as anything to pointing this out – it would be impossible to find Harte guilty.'

'Besides,' said the tenth juror, 'there's the difference where motive is concerned. Harte only wanted four hundred pounds –'

'Only,' echoed the ninth juror, disagreeably.

'I don't see that, I'm afraid.' This was the second juror speaking. 'Both of them wanted the money to go away with the woman they loved.'

There was a silence while each of them considered that. 'No,' said the foreman at last, decisively. 'I still think we can't convict Harte. Suppose we put it to the vote now, see how we stand . . .'

It was only a quarter of an hour later that they filed back into the jury-box again, to return a verdict of Not Guilty.

TUESDAY, after the verdict

It was late when Antony got home that night. There had been Harte's gratitude to cope with, and after that a session with Derek (amused) and Geoffrey (frankly jubilant) before he left the court; and then Chief Inspector Sykes waylaid him in the corridor. Gibbs was waiting at the back of the hall when he let himself into the house in Kempenfeldt Square. 'Sir Nicholas went upstairs some time ago,' he said, in a tone that carried the implication as plainly as words could have done that it was the duty of a host to be there to receive his guests. Antony, who was more tired than he would have cared to admit, received the information with a grin, and began to ascend the stairs rather more slowly than was his usual custom. Tuesday night, of course, Uncle Nick's night for dining with them; not that he would have expected anything else in the circumstances, whatever day of the week it had been.

Jenny met him in the upstairs hall. 'We've heard about the case, Antony. Mr. Halloran phoned, I don't know how he always seems to know everything.' Her anxious eyes scanned his face, but he was safe with Jenny; he knew from experience that she would never refer to his tiredness, or the awkward way he moved when his shoulder was painful. For one reason and another he could never bear to remember . . . 'I'm afraid you'll have to resign yourself to telling Uncle Nick about it.' He grimaced at that, but made no other comment. 'He's curious,' said Jenny simply.

In the living-room, Sir Nicholas was already well into his second glass of sherry. 'I understand,' he said, looking at his nephew in a benevolent way that was most probably misleading, 'that right has once more triumphed.'

'Well, I think so.' He sat down himself, opposite his uncle, and waited until Jenny had placed a glass at his elbow. Then he said, 'Father William's evidence couldn't be brought out in court, but once the police start looking they'll uncover what there is to know in short order.'

'Did Chief Inspector Sykes tell you that?'

'How did you know – '

'My dear boy, it was obvious he would want to talk to you.'

'Well, he did say that, more or less. But – this will amuse you, Uncle Nick – he also told me that the police were already suspicious of Blake over the murder of Lady Bowling. He thought they'd expedite action on that, and then look into our affair at their leisure.'

'Yes, well, it's all very satisfactory, I suppose. But I do wish you found it possible to get your effects in a rather less sensational manner.'

Antony smiled at that, and picked up his glass. 'It was Garfield's sensation, not mine,' he pointed out. 'If my very decorous examination of the witness didn't satisfy old Conroy – '

'That was clever of you,' Sir Nicholas conceded. 'I wonder how you got Garfield's co-operation.'

'Well, I said *if* I could get Blake to contradict flatly what Bowling and Wyatt had told the court, then in the interests of justice – '

'Was it really quite as simple as that?'

'I didn't get away without a serious lecture on the folly of starting things I couldn't finish, but apart from that – '

Sir Nicholas was following his own train of thought. 'In its way it was a master stroke,' he said. 'His cross-examination, I am sure, was far more cold-blooded than anything you could have achieved.'

'Now, how do I take that?'

'You must decide for yourself. Meanwhile, there is something else I should like to know. How were you sure enough of your facts to engage in the very dangerous manoeuvres you performed this morning in court?'

'I knew about Blake, of course, from Father William.'

'I am speaking of your examination of Bowling and Wyatt.'

'Bowling had told me . . . he's another chap with a conscience, Uncle Nick. As for Wyatt, if you'd seen him on Saturday, as I did, you'd have known he was hiding something. I couldn't see what else it could be, particularly as he tried to deceive me about the time he left the drawing-room, and when he thought I knew, and wasn't just guessing, he didn't want to risk a perjury charge.'

'Your tactics came dangerously near to blackmail, Antony.'

'Well . . . perhaps. But as far as the court was concerned I was just ribbing him about the difference between his own description of himself as a financier, and his activities as a money-lender.'

Sir Nicholas closed his eyes for a moment, but otherwise ignored this descent into colloquialism. 'You will forgive me for saying,' he remarked coldly, 'that I think you succeeded beyond your deserts.'

'It's Harte's deserts we should be concerned with, not mine.'

His uncle conceded the point with an inclination of his head. 'There is one other matter that was not cleared up in court, upon which I must confess to a certain amount of curiosity,' he said. Jenny, who thought this was almost certainly an understatement, hid a smile by picking up her glass. 'Wyatt said that George DeLisle was writing letters. What happened to them?'

'That's something we can't possibly know for sure unless Blake confesses. I think he took them away with him to create the impression that George DeLisle had died much earlier than was in fact the case. At a pinch he could have got Lady Bowling to give him an alibi for the earlier time.'

'That leads to another question: why did he kill her? According to you, he loved her.'

'Yes, but I think she had become suspicious during the last few days of her life. Sir Leonard said she had been *distrait* ever since she appeared in court.'

'But to *kill* her,' Jenny protested.

'When it came to a question of his own safety . . . remember, he hadn't planned to murder George

DeLisle and was probably pretty appalled by what had happened. He thought everyone had gone to bed when he heard the trio from the drawing-room go upstairs. And that was rash of him, he can only just have missed being seen by the butler. As for Lady Bowling, I expect he knew he had lost her anyway.'

'That's why he forgave Eleanor and their engagement was on again,' said Jenny, suddenly enlightened. 'If he was engaged to her nobody could suspect him of carrying on with Lady Bowling.'

'I'm afraid that was probably the original intention of the engagement, as a blind. Poor girl, she's the one who started everything, and the one who's come worst out of it in the end.'

'It will be a shock to her, of course,' said Jenny thoughtfully. 'But didn't you think she was probably at least half in love with Malcolm Harte, and that was why she came to you in the first place?'

'Yes, I think I did. But he isn't even half in love with her, and what her parents would say – '

'She might not care about that. Anyway, he's out of that other girl's clutches.'

'I agree. I don't think he'll go back to Mary Reynolds.'

'I don't think he'll want to go back to work for Henry DeLisle either. I was thinking it was a happy ending, or almost, but what on earth will become of him, Antony?'

'Didn't I tell you? Father William is offering him a job.'

Sir Nicholas was moved to protest. 'Now, really, Antony – '

'He runs a perfectly respectable, genuine business, Uncle Nick, and Harte will never be any the wiser, any more than Geraldine was when she worked for him. And I don't suppose he'll be quite so hard up as he was

191

in the past, because whatever you say about Father William, he's not ungenerous.'

'This passion for arranging other people's lives,' said Sir Nicholas, and sighed. But when he seemed to be about to continue Jenny – thinking he had had enough latitude for one evening – put down her glass firmly and got to her feet.

'The chicken will be burned to a cinder,' she announced. 'And really, Uncle Nick, as far as arranging other people's lives is concerned, you know it's no more than you would do yourself.'

Sir Nicholas's portrayal of a martyr, misunderstood by his nearest and dearest, lasted no longer than it took her to get dinner on the table.